PERIL IN THE AIR!

Perowne singled out a 109 diving to his starboard. He banked, tried to judge deflection, and fired, but the enemy continued to half-roll towards him. He fired again. The two aircraft looped and rolled, and for an instant he exposed his Spitfire's belly to the 109's fire, and his aircraft juddered violently as the cannon shells struck the hull; then, with sweat pouring down his face, his arms and legs aching, and a fierce pain thudding in his brain, he twisted further in the roll and the dogfight continued . . .

Squadron 1
Sons of the Morning
MATTHEW HOLDEN

SPHERE BOOKS LIMITED
30/32 Gray's Inn Road, London WC1X 8JL

First published in Sphere Books Ltd 1978
Reprinted 1979
Copyright © Matthew Holden 1978

TRADE
MARK

Set in Intertype Times

Printed in Great Britain by
Hazell Watson & Viney Ltd
Aylesbury, Bucks

CHAPTER ONE

Six of them waited for the dawn to spread over the Dunkirk beach. They crouched beside the ruined Renault truck with cold gnawing their bones, and the young private still moaned from the shrapnel wound in his thigh. Sergeant Gow glanced at their faces in the grey light: twenty-four hours earlier there had been eleven men under his command, the remains of B Company, but four had been lost during the confused fighting to cover the last miles before Dunkirk and one more lay three feet under the sand beyond the truck, his rifle marking the grave. Gow noted the weariness of the survivors, and more than this, the apparent resignation that they were finished. Only Corporal Keevin showed signs of spirit. Gow lifted his head at the sound of the droning engine, and tried to wipe the sand from his eyes as he squinted towards the east. The moan rose and fell, but steadily became louder and more insistent until Gow could detect the black aircraft dots against the early morning sky. 'Three, maybe four,' he muttered. 'Here they come again.'

'Bastards,' said Keevin. His voice seemed almost matter-of-fact. Gow spoke louder. 'Under the truck – come on, move!' Now he could hear the rising rattle of machine-gun fire; he turned to the young private and dragged him beneath the Renault chassis, ignoring the boy's whimpering, and he lay close beside him, feeling his violent shivering against his thigh.

The Messerschmitts came in low, unafraid and flaunting their apparent invulnerability. Short bursts from their guns merged into a deafening clatter, and then the first shadow swept above the truck. Gow could see the next aircraft fifty yards up the beach, close enough for him to notice the oil smears on the machine's ugly yellow belly and the flash of white of the pilot's face in the square cockpit canopy. Two sudden explosions roared from somewhere to the left, pierced by screams and shouts, and the noise of another aircraft blasted louder; this time the bullets ripped into the Renault – an abrupt cacophony sounding like tearing calico – and Gow instinctively pressed his face hard into the sand. The Me 109 thundered on. Gow lay still for a moment, smelling his own sweat and faint cordite and the stink of the petrol-soaked sand beneath his cheek.

'Harry's bought it.' Gow turned in the direction of the voice then wearily lifted himself and crawled towards the tail of the wrecked Renault. Two of his men were crouched beside a third who lay on his face with arms outstretched and gaping holes across his back. 'We've time to bury him before they come again.' Gow crawled from beneath the truck and stood, searching in his pockets for a cigarette, even though he knew he'd smoked the last two days before. Keevin pushed his own packet forward.

Around them the remains of the British Expeditionary Force were beginning to recover from the latest Luftwaffe attack, and lines of troops had already formed again in the shallow water, waiting for the boats to lift them away. Smoke rose steadily from Dunkirk, bringing with it the cloying stench of burning rubber. Another Luftwaffe attack seemed to be taking place further along the beach towards La Panne.

'They'll be back soon,' said Gow, still savouring the cigarette. 'Aye,' muttered Keevin, his face already looking towards the sky. 'They do what they bloody well like while we sit on our fannies,' Keevin added. 'What

I'd like to bleeding know is what the hell the RAF thinks it's doing. Christ Almighty, we see nothing of them. It's been days since we even saw a Spitfire – and then it were in a ditch arse-end up like a bloody duck. Where's the rest of them flying Johnnies?' He flung away the cigarette in disgust. 'I'll tell you where. Back home, having breakfast, while we sit 'ere like pregnant bloody sows.' Gow reluctantly dropped the shred of his cigarette, and they turned to grasp the imploring outstretched arms of the dead man and drag him out onto the open sand.

Squadron-Leader Teddy Perowne pushed away his plate on the dispersal hut table. The kippers tasted foul, congealed from the time it had taken for them to be brought from the squadron mess. Perowne picked up his coffee mug and tried to swill the grease from his mouth, then, searching for his pipe in his flying jacket pocket, he sat back to study his pilots.

They waited for the early morning clouds to clear, and for their first mission to begin over Belgium: it would only be the third operational flight since the squadron moved down to Kent from Yorkshire forty-eight hours before. None of the pilots had so far seen the enemy; all knew that the first contact would almost inevitably be made within an hour or so. The squadron which they'd rushed to replace was decimated in the fighting over Belgium – seven out of eleven pilots shot down, five of them killed. Perowne had hoped for at least another month of training in Yorkshire, but, on this first day of June 1940, the Germans were allowing no time for leisurely RAF preparations, and the squadron would be thrown unready into battle. Perowne lit his pipe, the sound of the lighter rasping in the heavy silence of the dispersal hut, and his anxious thoughts continued.

Spitfire flying hours were minimal. Three of the pilots

– Joe Caton, George Barclay and Sergeant Dundas – had arrived from their Operational Training Unit only two weeks before. Of the others, only two pilots – the New Zealander, 'Lex' MacIntyre, and Simon Tattersall – could be judged reasonably proficient, having been in the Cambridge University Air Squadron before going to their Initial Training Wing, then Cranwell and the OTU. The squadron itself was only six weeks old and still understrength, with nine pilots rather than the establishment figure of twelve. Now five of the nine waited 'on state' with Perowne for the telephone to ring and the order to fly. The Squadron-Leader appraised them one by one, his pipe sagging from the corner of his mouth and the smoke mingling with the thick cigarette haze in the hut.

Joe Caton sat forward with his elbows on his knees, his dark head lowered, fingers fiddling with the table-leg, and Perowne could see the boy's thumb nail digging into the soft wood to make a pattern. His puppy lay asleep at his feet. Joe was the quiet one – friendly but reserved; it was difficult to know what he thought or felt, but he seemed intelligent – perhaps excessively so, thought Perowne; intelligence often brought imagination, and a pilot who thought too much was likely to lose his nerve.

Joe seemed so different from Simon Tattersall, his room-mate, who now sat beside him with his feet on the table; Simon – solid and always laughing, his boxer's build and strength revealing the sporting prowess which had earned him a Cambridge Blue. Perowne's glance shifted to the trio sitting on the far side of the room: Sergeant Jones and Pilot Officer Marder were comparative strangers, but Perowne suspected that Marder might be over-cocky and in need of curbing; Sergeant Dundas seemed capable, with a healthy youthful acceptance of whatever might be round the corner.

Perowne's thoughts flitted momentarily to the men 'off state' – Lex, his second in command, with a fiery recklessness that matched his ginger hair; George Barclay, serious, with an analytical brain and an almost frightening attitude to efficiency; Sergeant Hyde, anxious to please. Time would tell, if time allowed.

Perowne jumped at the sudden sound of the telephone. Simon swung his boots from the table and reached for the instrument and the harsh ringing ceased. Perowne took the receiver from Simon's outstretched hand and listened to the calm voice of the Controller. Scramble. Destination French-Belgian coast. Mission to cover embarkation activity.

'Scramble boys!' shouted Perowne. Simon and Marder were already pushing through the door, the rest close behind. 'Come on! Let's see how quick we can get aloft. For Christ's sake move!'

Keevin smoothed the last shovelful of sand over the grave and then the Luftwaffe came again, this time a bomber and two fighters. The corporal flung himself beneath the Renault; Sergeant Gow remained standing by the battered vehicle. He saw the eruptions of sand and soil further along the dunes, and watched the Messerschmitts skimming just above the sea to machine-gun the lines of troops standing in the water. Gow turned his head and watched the disappearing aircraft; Keevin told him that the boy had died at last, and they began to dig again; the corporal continued to grumble at their lack of RAF protection.

Perowne's hands rested gently on the column. He checked his mirror again and glanced to right and left. The six Spitfires flew in two V sections, with Perowne

9

leading the first, and with the second only a few yards behind. He noted with satisfaction that his pilots were holding position according to regulations with one 12-yard wing span between them, on a level line. Perowne flicked on his R/T and hoped his pilots had remembered to switch their sets to 'receive' rather than 'transmit'.

'Hello, Orange Leader, Piper Leader calling. Well done, Simon, but keep looking behind.' Simon, leading the second section, replied immediately, 'OK Piper Leader. We'll guard your tail.'

Twelve thousand feet below, the sea was flecked with white, and Perowne could see three small boats moving in single file towards England; ahead he could see the French coast, and further to the east, black clouds were boiling like a thunderstorm.

'Jesus.' Simon's voice came over the R/T again. 'That must be Dunkirk. Just look at it!'

'Don't natter. We'll climb now. Angels X for X-Ray. Steer 090 degrees – zero, nine, zero. And watch for Huns in the sun.' Perowne banked eastwards and pulled back the control column. The altimeter needle crept upwards to the specified 20,000 feet. Behind him, Simon's section followed, still in close formation, and ahead the smoke of Dunkirk reached up towards them.

Joe Caton felt vomit in his throat. His stomach stretched tight, and sweat from his fingers soaked his silk gloves as he clutched the stick; his thighs were shivering against the seat. He caught himself muttering, 'Look behind, behind, behind,' and his eyes darted from the mirror to the tip of Simon's starboard wing as he tried to keep formation. A grey line streaked past his cockpit, then another, and at the same moment, a Spitfire in front of him in the first section exploded into orange flame, and the R/T began to babble.

'Huns! Huns!'

'Break right!'

'I'm hit! God, I'm hit!'

Joe flung his Spitfire to starboard, and another line of tracer whipped above his head. He dived towards Dunkirk; he'd still to see an enemy aircraft. His speed increased as he screwed his head from side to side searching for the Messerschmitts, but the sky seemed empty and he gradually pulled back the stick. The Spitfire responded and Joe began to climb again, banking first one way then the other, his legs like jelly as he pushed the rudder bar, and sweat trickled down his chin. Out of the corner of his eye, he suddenly saw a Spitfire spiralling downwards. Below him the beach of Dunkirk swayed from side to side, and he noticed the wounded Spitfire pull abruptly from its spiral to crash in an eruption of spray not far from the shore.

Perowne's quiet voice sounded close to Joe's ear. 'Orange Leader. Piper here. We'll reform. Angels 15 . . .' Joe almost sobbed with relief at the ending to his loneliness, and he began to search for the other survivors.

Sergeant Gow and Corporal Keevin waded through the shallows, the water splashing cold over their chests as they pushed as fast as they could to the Spitfire. Other troops were running down the beach behind them to join the rescue; the aircraft lay half-covered by the sea, one wing skywards as if pointing. Keevin, smaller and more nimble, reached the Spitfire first. He hauled himself onto the fuselage to grasp the half-open cockpit. 'The bugger won't budge.' He helped Gow up beside him, and the Sergeant's huge hands heaved the perspex cover to gain six more inches. 'It'll do,' muttered Gow, and he reached inside.

Gow took the pilot to the shore, finding him light in his arms, and laid him on the sand. He ripped off the flying helmet to reveal blond curly hair, damp with sweat.

'Christ,' exclaimed Keevin. 'He's only a lad.'

'No younger than some of our lot.'

'Maybe. But yon's a helluva great machine for a lad to fly.'

The eyes flickered open, green and wide with fear and pain, and the boy began to whimper. Gow bent to catch the words before turning to Keevin. 'He says his back hurts.'

'Aye, look, there's blood. What's he saying now?'

'Something about he's sorry.'

'What the hell for?'

'Because he's not so good at it yet.' Gow straightened and added: 'Nor will he ever be. He's gone.' His clumsy large fingers closed the boy's eyes. 'Come on – we'll bury him with ours.'

Perowne walked stiff-legged back into the dispersal hut. Joe and Simon stood for a moment longer, looking at the skyline above the beeches and listening for the sound of an aircraft, then they turned to follow the Squadron-Leader. Perowne cradled the mug of tea in his hands and watched Joe as he ladled sugar into his: the boy's hands were still shaking. 'Cheer up Joe.'

'I'm all right. But three gone. Three!'

'Dundas might still make it. You say you saw a Spit go down at Dunkirk – that must've been Marder, and he may have got out after the crash. We know Jones bought it. But he may be the only one.' Perowne took out his pipe and knocked free the ash remaining from the last smoke before the sortie; through the open door, he could see the mechanics refuelling the Spitfires, ready

12

for another flight. One gone at least. Perhaps three. Half the pilots in the mission – and with none of them firing a single burst.

Dundas returned twelve minutes later with his aircraft drinking its last drop of fuel, and with a dozen bullet holes in the fuselage. Jones was listed as killed in action; Marder was reported missing. Perowne completed the necessary paperwork before lunch then flew with the second flight during the afternoon: Joe and Simon were placed 'off state'.

The weather remained clear over the Channel. This time, the Spitfires flew in two sections of two, and Perowne sensed immediately that the pair formation allowed far greater freedom. George flew on his left, acting as his Number Two; Lex and Hyde followed close behind, and with the absence of another aircraft on the right flank, Perowne felt that some of the burden of having to keep tight formation had been removed. Now they could spend more time searching for the enemy.

He led the sections along the beaches towards Dunkirk. He glanced below for a moment and noted the files of men reaching out into the shallows.

Hyde spoke over the R/T. 'Poor sods. We can't do much for them.'

Lex broke in, 'Piper Leader. I see a Spit in the water. Shall I look?'

'OK Lex. Take your Number Two and we'll cover.'

The two Spitfires peeled away, made a low run over the beach and then returned. Lex reported, 'It's Marder's number. Cockpit hood seems open. They must've got him out.'

'Aircraft! Coming low inland!' Hyde almost shouted over the R/T.

'I see them. Climb, boys! Climb!' Perowne pulled back the stick, and the three aircraft followed. He ob-

13

served with relief the way they moved smoothly back into echelon formation, and at the same time he searched south to catch the Germans again. Two aircraft were flying low, their shadows racing across the fields and over the ditches towards the dunes. He glanced around him and saw no other enemy, noted the altimeter needle at 12,000 feet, and spoke again to his pilots. 'That'll do. Let's go.' He pushed the column forward and pressed the rudder-bar to twist into a half-roll and begin his dive.

Almost immediately, he felt the nagging anxiety replaced by acute anticipation. The enemy aircraft grew larger and he recognized the blunt noses and broad straight-tapered wings of Heinkel 111's; they made good targets for fighters, with only three hand-aimed machine-guns, or so it was said.

Perowne checked that he'd thumbed forward the safety catch on his gun as the leading Heinkel loomed in his sights. The enemy seemed unaware of the Spitfire's approach. Deflection would be minimal. The gap closed rapidly. He checked his mirror one last time, saw George tight on his tail, then pressed his thumb on the button. His Spitfire vibrated, his tracer curved away to the right of the leading bomber, and the Heinkel began to swerve. He pressed the button again, and this time, lights sparkled along the fuselage. Smoke suddenly gushed, and the Heinkel tilted into a vicious death dive; Perowne guessed he had hit the pilot. He eased his Spitfire back into a rising half-roll, twisting to look over his left shoulder as he climbed.

The Heinkel plunged in a smoke-shrouded spiral; George was banking upwards to the south; no sign of the others. Perowne levelled at 5,000 feet, and watched as the enemy aircraft hit the ground in a massive, silent explosion; he'd seen no parachutes, and anyway, the

Heinkel had been flying too low. He had killed five men, yet he felt no sense of being an executioner, nor did he enjoy jubilation. Perhaps some reaction would follow. At the moment, it all seemed too mechanical. He climbed, with George on his tail again, searching for the others without success. 'Hello Orange Two. Any sign of Yellow Section?'

George answered immediately. 'I saw them chasing the other bandit. Heading south.'

South – that meant inland. Perowne swore to himself: Lex was asking for trouble. 'OK Orange Two,' he said. 'We'll patrol another circuit, then go home.'

Lex returned a few minutes after Perowne and George. He came alone. He flew low over the airfield, turning in a slow victory roll, then banked above the beeches to come in to land. He walked smiling from his Spitfire, unfastening his parachute, and Perowne went to meet him.

'I got the sod!' Lex exclaimed. 'I had to chase the blighter, but I got him in the end.'

'Where's Hyde?'

'Isn't he back? I thought he must be with you. We both went after the Heinkel, then I looked round and he'd gone. I thought he must've turned back, so I went on alone.'

'Lex, you're a bloody fool.' Perowne had stopped walking; he spoke quietly so that the others waiting outside dispersal wouldn't hear.

Lex stared at him, a frown on his pale freckled face. 'Why, for Christ's sake?'

'For going on a chase over France. Orders were to patrol, not to shoot off inland: especially with a novice as your Number Two.'

'Hell, man. I got the Hun, didn't I? That's what they

pay us for. Hyde'll soon be here. You worry too much – like a broody hen.'

Hyde had still to return at nightfall, hours after his aircraft would have run out of fuel. Perowne still hoped the telephone would ring to say the sergeant had landed elsewhere, perhaps a coastal airfield, but no message came. He sat in his room, the air thick with his pipe smoke, alternately adding a few sentences to the letter to Anna and scribbling diagrams on the pad – aircraft formations, in pairs, Vs, echelon, line astern . . . Jones, Marder, Hyde. Jones for certain. Three men gone out of nine. Three aircraft lost against two German. Perhaps Lex was right – he mustn't be a broody hen. He wrote a few more words to Anna and tried to switch his thoughts to the silkiness of her dark hair, the warmth of her skin, the responsiveness of her body, and then his mind returned to the Dunkirk beaches, and to the long lines of men reaching out into the sea, helpless and waiting for God only knew what.

Joe caught the waiter's attention on his third attempt and ordered another bottle. They sat round the table in the crowded London restaurant – Joe, Simon, George and Lex, celebrating the latter's victory; at least, thought Joe, Lex and Simon seemed to be celebrating. George was polite as always; Joe had been reluctant to come, but even more unwilling to spend the evening alone in his room, without Simon's cheerful presence. He glanced around him at the other tables, at the women who looked so clean and healthy and fresh, the men smart, and he smelt the food and perfume and cigar-smoke; he remembered the horror of those few seconds this morning with the Dunkirk desolation revolving below him, and became conscious of the sweat in his palms as he reached for his wine glass.

'But you should've seen it,' Lex was saying.

'God, man, we've heard it all before,' said Simon, grinning. 'You wait – after tomorrow, you won't be the only one to crow.'

Tomorrow. Joe set down his drink, trying to prevent the wine from trembling in the glass. He said, 'The old man seems worried.'

'Hell, he's always bleating,' Lex commented.

'He's a good bloke,' said Simon.

'Of course he is. But he natters too much. We can look after ourselves.'

George spoke, slowly and carefully as he always did. 'It rather seems Arthur Hyde couldn't.'

'And just what do you mean by that?'

'Nothing, Lex. Nothing. Nor could Billy Marder or Jones. We all have a lot to learn.'

Joe looked up quickly. George was smiling, self-assured and with an almost indulgent expression as he studied Lex. Simon laughed, 'Come on, let's talk about something else. Better still, let's have a frolic. I fancy the blonde over there.'

Lex was already on his feet, and the two of them pushed between the tables, racing each other for the same pretty girl – who already sat with a sober-faced escort. Joe managed to smile, then he re-filled his glass, pushed the bottle to George, and tried not to think about tomorrow.

CHAPTER TWO

Smooth clouds stretched beneath them, and above spread the long thin trail of black, which Perowne had encountered above Brighton and which would lead them to the blazing oil dumps at Dunkirk. He checked his mirror again. Once more, the squadron flew according to regulations in two V sections, himself leading the first, this time with Lex heading the second. He glanced above trying to spot enemy aircraft lying in the filthy Dunkirk smoke, and his apprehension rose steadily: silhouetted against the white cloud below, his six Spitfires would be a perfect target.

He flicked his R/T to transmit. 'Hello Orange Leader. We'll start a descent.' His Spitfire began its shallow dive, and the clouds wisped by his cockpit to give welcome cover; only two minutes later, he broke through the canopy. He eased back the stick to fly level for a moment beneath the white layer, and he checked the positions of his pilots: all were maintaining close formation.

Ahead lay Dunkirk, the root of the huge oily tendril which curled right across the Channel. Land rapidly approached, and he dropped steadily lower before banking to begin the coastal patrol; he checked his altimeter – 2,000 feet – and spoke over the R/T again. 'Piper Leader here. We'll stick at Angels Two. It'll give the chaps below a boost to see us. But for goodness sake, keep your eyes open for Huns above.'

The six aircraft roared in their perfect formation along the edge of the beaches, and Perowne immediately noted the vastly increased activity since the previous day. Seawards, a destroyer moved out of the pall of smoke, lying deep in the water, her decks crowded with troops. Around the warship circled fishing smacks and paddle steamers and dozens of small boats, all packed with troops as well. Men were still standing in the water, like half-submerged fences at right-angles to the beach. Bomb craters showed as fresh ochre circles in the lighter tan of sand, and around these holes twisted the lines of soldiers.

Perowne observed the stacks of equipment and abandoned vehicles, and even the rifles piled into huge heaps, and everywhere groups of men waiting for deliverance. He could see the upturned faces and arms waving as he flashed above them, and then a curtain of black fell across his cockpit perspex as he swept into the greasy smoke of Dunkirk. He emerged two seconds later and immediately banked in a climb. Flames licked the darkness below, and as the Spitfire rose, he could see beyond the smoke to the scores of wrecks which were littering the shallows, masts or hulls sticking obscenely out of the water. Through them moved a second destroyer and other vessels which were pulling strings of Thames river craft and fragile dinghies, and as Perowne glanced in their direction, he suddenly noted the eruptions of foam around them. He immediately called Lex. 'Orange Leader. Bandits to starboard. Bombing the destroyer.'

'I see it, Piper Leader. I'll take Orange Section, OK?'

'OK, Orange Leader.' Perowne looked over his shoulder and saw the second section peeling to starboard.

Lex, always eager, shouted over the R/T, 'Tallyho!' And the three Spitfires disappeared into the murk.

'Lucky sods.' Simon's goodnatured complaint came over the radio. 'Heaven help us if Lex gets another.'

'Stop prattling, Yellow Two.'

19

'Bogey. High to port. I think they could be Huns.' Joe sounded calm, his voice restrained. Perowne searched upwards to his left and after a moment he located the cluster of dots. At the same moment, the dots separated as they began to dive.

'Climb! Climb!' Perowne pulled the stick into the pit of his stomach and pressed hard on the rudder bar to angle his Spitfire in the direction of the approaching enemy. The two groups would meet head-on, reducing the Spitfires into a minimum-sized target which might cancel the disparity in numbers. He boosted his speed to the maximum, and his Spitfire propeller clawed the smoke-laden air: he spared a moment to check the other two aircraft in his section – Simon had reacted vigorously and had drawn level, Joe flew slightly to the rear.

Tracer dropped towards them, seeming to flow slowly at first, then suddenly accelerating the last few yards. Too high and too early. Perowne kept his thumb poised while the shape of the Messerschmitt became etched sharper in his reflector sight. Tracer from Simon's Spitfire flashed past him, and Perowne fired at almost the same moment, so it was impossible to judge which of them hit the enemy. The Messerschmitt's starboard wing burst from the fuselage, and the enemy machine hurtled sideways beneath Perowne's. Another loomed before his sights, and he fired but could see nothing of the effect before he found the sky clear in front of him. He banked to port.

'Piper Leader! Hun! On your tail!'

Perowne twisted his machine into a vicious half-roll, pushing his throttle wide open and pulling back his stick into the near vertical power dive. An aircraft blacked his cockpit for a moment, but he'd escaped. He levelled in time to see the Messerschmitt being chased in a shallow dive by a Spitfire; he recognized the number, and blessed Joe for the warning. Joe must have stuck right behind to give protection, he thought. Good flying. He searched the sky again, bending forward in his cockpit as he looked above, then he noted the drooping fuel needle, and turned for home.

The Me 109 reached the base of its dive and began to level over the waves. Joe kept his throttle wide open, but the enemy's greater diving speed drew the 109 further away, and already the German was crossing the Belgian coast. Joe throttled back and banked away, and as he did so he became aware of the painful tightness of his fingers on the stick; he licked his parched lips and struggled to breathe normally. Joe realized that for a few seconds when the Me 109 had exposed its belly to dive on Perowne, he'd had the power to kill a man. Yet his thumb had remained above the button; he tried to explain why to himself but failed. Instead, the driving sense of isolation swept over him as he searched round the sky. He was alone, a target for the enemy; once again, he clamped his teeth together, and his fingers gripped hard on the stick, seeking reassurance from his aircraft.

'Hello, Yellow Three. Hey Joe! I'm below you.'

Joe looked beneath him on either side but could see nothing, Then, banking slightly, he saw Simon's Spitfire flying just to the rear. He grinned with relief and tried to keep his voice emotionless. 'Hello Simon. Nice to see you. My fuel's low. Should we go home?'

'OK, you lazy sod.'

Six miles farther across the Channel, two more Spitfires were also heading for the squadron airfield. Lex glanced in his mirror and saw George still on his tail. Good old George. Lex sat back in his cramped seat and again saw

21

the Dornier plummeting in flames, and he rehearsed the flippant sentences with which he'd describe his triumph – his second kill. But Lex felt no joy, simply a release from the secret terror which had gripped him throughout the sortie and throughout the previous day. He experienced momentary escape from the need to be brave, yet he remembered the scream stabbing his ears which he'd believed to be his own until he'd seen Dundas's Spitfire twisting downwards, and he shivered with fresh convulsions at the thought of the Sergeant struggling in a frenzy to prise back the cockpit canopy as he fell. His lips moved as he whispered, 'Christ, it could've been me. Me, for Christ's sake.' And not even the thought of his second kill, and the congratulations he would receive, could wipe out the horror.

Lex only knew that his pretence of bravery must be maintained, and another kill inflicted so that his sham reputation could be confirmed. He must kill to thrust aside his fear of being killed. Below him lay Dover with the lace ribbon of cliffs which signalled temporary safety; he flew on, over the fields of Kent, still trying to smother his fear. He located the woods to the north of the airfield, received permission to land, and came in low giving the re-arm signal over the dispersal area – a sideslip from side to side – knowing this would please the aircrew waiting below, since they'd know he'd been in action. Yet as he undertook this manoeuvre, his fear surged stronger: re-arming served as recognition that soon another sortie would begin, and the hell would be repeated.

Perowne asked the pilots to stay for a few minutes after the mess dinner that night. He walked to the fireplace, resting his glass on the beer-stained mantle and knocking his pipe in the grate before turning to speak. The pilots were sitting in the dilapidated armchairs or squatting on the drab RAF carpet, glasses in hands. He waited for the chatter to ebb and then he spoke, trying to keep the anxiety from his voice.

'We've had two days over Dunkirk, and we've downed four enemy aircraft. But Jones and Dundas have gone for certain. We know Marder crash-landed near the beach and he might be OK. But we've heard nothing of Hyde, and I'm afraid we would have done by now – at the least, he must be behind enemy lines. So we've lost two and perhaps three, or maybe even four.'

He glanced at each of the silent pilots. Joe sat closest to him, staring into his glass; George was leaning forward, carefully filling his pipe; Lex fiddled with the corner of a magazine, and Perowne felt a moment's irritation – the New Zealander seemed bored; Simon met Perowne's eyes, gave a quick, reassuring grin and said, 'We'll improve for you. Just wait.'

'There's no time for waiting. We have to pull our fingers out on the next sortie.'

Lex shuffled impatiently. 'What more can we do? Hell, I've shot down two, haven't I?'

'Of course, Lex. But two aircraft from your sections have gone, one for each of your kills.'

'That's not my bloody fault.'

Joe interrupted quietly, 'Let's hear what the old man has to say, Lex.'

Perowne smiled slightly – an 'old man' at twenty-seven. He began to discuss tactics, and the pilots contributed, especially George. They'd try a looser V formation, so reducing the close watch that had to be kept on distances between them. Then Perowne repeated the points which the pilots should already have known as well as their own names, and which couldn't be repeated often enough – look out behind, see the enemy before he sees you, try to be up-sun whenever possible, always make sure you can use the Spitfire's greater manouevr- ability, avoid any chance of the Me 109 dropping into a shallow dive since the Hun then gained the speed advantage, don't waste ammunition, don't become so involved in attacking an aircraft that you forget to guard against another's intervention . . . As he spoke Perowne examined the reaction of the pilots to the familiar maxims. Joe watched him in return with ap- parent interest; Simon continued to meet his eyes; George even took notes; Lex doodled with his finger-tip in a puddle of beer on the arm of his chair.

Perowne finished. 'One last thing. There's too much talking on the R/T. Especially you, Simon.' He smiled. 'Save your gossip for the girls.'

'OK – you find me the girls first. Come on. If you've finished being a schoolmaster, I'll buy you a drink.'

Within five minutes, Lex was sitting at the battered piano, and the songs had started. The sound of the cheerful and tuneless music followed Perowne down the bare corridor to his room. He picked up his pen to con- tinue the letter to Anna, re-reading the last words writ- ten the previous night. 'One or two teething troubles have to be sorted out, but experience will settle every- thing. I'm lucky to have such a grand crowd.' He stared at the page then started a new paragraph. 'I miss you, my darling. And I haven't forgotten that 8 June is our anniversary – only five days to go.'

Less than a week. Perowne wondered almost dispas- sionately how many of those pilots singing in the mess would still be alive. Did he expect to be? He remem- bered last year's wedding anniversary, their first, and even recalled the day of the week – Thursday. He'd taken Anna to their favourite Chelsea restaurant just round the corner from the flat, and they'd walked back slightly tipsy, leaning for a moment on the smooth Embankment wall to watch the river gliding past, then hurrying back to the flat and impatiently to bed. Later, he'd opened the window, and the sweet scent of Anna's body had been replaced by the blossom from the tree-lined street. Now if he opened the window, he'd probably be able to smell the faint stench of Dunkirk, reaching across the Channel along the trail which the squadron would fly again tomorrow.

Pilot Officer Arthur Grant, a replacement who arrived at the squadron early next morning, died during the afternoon in further fighting over Dunkirk; another replacement, Sergeant Johnny Wright, shot down a Junkers 87 'Stuka', finishing off the crippled dive-bomber after Perowne had inflicted severe damage. Perowne gave him official credit for the kill. Simon claimed a 'probable'; Lex returned with fifteen bullet holes in his fuselage, and he cloaked his fear by saying each hole would be mended with a swastika patch, since he would soon have fifteen victims.

Joe landed ten minutes after the others. He taxied onto the grass and sat for a moment in the silence of his cockpit. He took his hands from the stick, stretched his tensed fingers, then took off his glove and placed the palm of his hand against the perspex, welcoming the warmth of the sun. The nose of the Spitfire rose high in front of him, and the sight and feel of the solid machine gave him strength: he slid back the hood to smell the fresh air mingled with the reek of fuel, and wearily he climbed into the open.

Perowne flew to Uxbridge, (headquarters of 11 Group Fighter Command) during the evening. He and other selected squadron-leaders had been summoned for a briefing by the Group Commander. They gathered in

Keith Park's spacious office and listened while the quiet-spoken New Zealander told them that Operation Dynamo, the evacuation from Dunkirk, would end tomorrow, 4 June. Results were excellent: the bulk of the BEF had been brought home. But pressure on the RAF would remain, and would probably even intensify. German forces were massing behind the Somme for the thrust into France; Hugh Dowding, Fighter Command Chief, was resisting appeals to send more squadrons to French airfields, but French calls for help were increasingly insistent and could not be totally denied, and British troops still fighting alongside their allies would need all possible cover.

Park ran his hand over his thin, pointed face and tugged his clipped moustache in an anxious gesture. 'Squadrons will still be based in England as far as possible, but they'll have to operate daily over France. Fuel problems will be obvious, but we're establishing depots on French soil for replenishment during the day.' Park looked intently at the assembled officers. 'Your squadrons will be those from this Group which will be immediately involved. I thought it best to give you fair warning. It's going to be tough for all of you.'

Next morning, Perowne's squadron flew its last patrol over Dunkirk. Almost incredibly, the herds of men waiting on the beaches had disappeared, and only scattered groups remained amongst the abandoned equipment. Perowne observed explosions just inland, probably mortar and field-gun fire, as the Germans pushed against the French perimeter. Vessels still moved close to the shore, manoeuvring between the forest of wrecks. The squadron saw no enemy aircraft; Lex expressed his disappointment over the radio, to which Perowne made no reply, and as they flew back over the Channel, the Squadron-Leader counted only three days to his wedding anniversary; perhaps he would make it. He banked his Spitfire and led the two sections low above a convoy, waggling his wings and seeing troops wave in answer from the crowded decks.

Gow watched the Spitfires dwindle into dots and disappear over the horizon, and the steady throb of the trawler's engines replaced the hornet whine of the aircraft. Around the Sergeant lay soldiers, sailors and civilians, all filthy, some covered with oil from the scummy water in which they had swum the last yards to the boat. Gow still clung to his rifle, and the weapon felt heavy in his aching arms. The trawler's gunwhale struck icy against his back, rubbing harshly through his sodden battledress tunic as the boat rose and fell. A private from his company lay slumped asleep against his right shoulder; Keevin squatted on his left, and Gow believed them to be the last survivors of his group.

Keevin stirred. 'It depends on them, I reckon.' The Corporal's voice was slurred with weariness.

'Who?' asked Gow.

'Them.' Keevin nodded in the direction of the horizon where the Spitfires had disappeared, then his helmet dropped forward again.

Gow sat with his legs straight, the spray drizzling on his skin, feeling the beat of the boat beneath him, and he remembered the pilot from the crashed Spitfire, and the frailty of the boy's body, and the whispered apology before the green eyes dulled in death.

CHAPTER THREE

Anna sat at the end of the second row, beside a stout lady who would be more in place at a comfortable talk at a local village institute. Together, they listened to the young doctor's lecture on emergency nursing in the event of bombing. 'Don't back away from dirt and filth. You'll see plenty, ladies and gentlemen. Blood and tissue and spilled guts are not pretty – and they smell. You'll have to get used to that.'

Outside the hall, the traffic murmured peacefully in the Chelsea street. Anna glanced at her neighbour: the woman's eyes stared to the front, fixing on a point somewhere above the doctor's head. 'If you come upon a casualty with his stomach laid open and his guts hanging out, simply push your hands into the wound and pack the guts back.'

Anna looked down at her hands – her long, slender fingers, still with traces of oil paint from her work at the studio earlier in the morning – fingers which Teddy said had the most sensitive and exciting touch that a man could ever wish. 'Hold your fists there to keep the guts in position, if you have nothing else. The mess and smell may revolt you, but that man needs his innards...'

She walked down to the embankment after the lecture and leant against the wall beside the Thames. The stone felt warm, and the breeze fluttered her long dark hair around her cheeks. She stared down at the water, watching the flotsam drifting up-river on the rising tide; then she heard sounds of cheering and the chug of multiple engines, and she looked towards Chelsea Bridge to see a line of small boats appearing round the bend. Gradually, they moved closer, and spectators on either bank welcomed them as they passed. A tug led the way, towing a dozen or so motor launches, and behind moved ordinary Thames river craft in groups of two and three. Anna noted their battered state, the scrapes and scars on the bright paintwork, and she realized this diminutive collection must form part of the evacuation fleet used at Dunkirk. Now the boats returned to their bankside moorings, in triumph.

A cloud passed over the sun, darkening the water and the brave colours on the river craft. Anna shivered and put her hands in her coat pockets. Her fingers found the temporary Red Cross armband which had just been issued to her, ready for the bombing of London, and she remembered again Teddy's joking words spoken after she'd told him of her decision. 'You'll never be needed as a nurse, my love. All my boys think as I do: if the Huns ever get as far as London, it'll be over our dead bodies.'

Teddy Perowne led his section up from the French refuelling field. Beneath him, the roads were crammed with refugees, some of whom fled into the ditches and fields as the three Spitfires roared above them, thinking the aircraft might be Stukas. The horizon hung shrouded with filthy black smoke. Glancing out of his cockpit, Perowne could see dead cattle, broken trees, shattered houses, abandoned vehicles, and at intervals, the flow of refugees parted for a moment to sweep beside the crumpled victims of Luftwaffe machine-gun raids. He banked for the coast, and a few moments later the Channel lay beneath them. He waited eagerly for the sight of England, and the soft sunlight shining on clean countryside.

'Hello, Piper Leader. Piper Leader. Orange Three here. My engine seems wonky.'

Perowne looked to port. Johnny Wright's aircraft had already started to slip behind. 'Hello, Orange Three. What's up Johnny?'

'Christ knows, sir. I'm losing power.'

'How do your instruments read?'

'Oil pressure sinking. Engine temperature rising fast. I can't keep up.'

'Don't fret, Johnny. We'll match your speed. Throttle well back in coarse pitch.' Perowne spoke to George, flying to starboard. 'Hello, Orange Two. Did you hear all that?'

'Roger, Piper Leader.'

'Climb and keep watch. Orbit if necessary. I'll cover Johnny's tail and watch for smoke.'

Perowne and George took up position above and behind the lame Spitfire. The sea stretched to an empty horizon, and Perowne estimated another five minutes before land would be sighted; nine or ten minutes should see the young Sergeant safe. Only three minutes later, Perowne noticed the first signs of black smoke wisping from the Spitfire in front of him. He said nothing until the smoke suddenly gushed thicker, then he glanced around him for enemy aircraft, noted George circling above, and spoke again to Wright. 'Johnny. You have smoke. I'm afraid you'll have to bale out. Your crate may explode. Don't worry – it's as easy as stepping off a log.'

'Yessir!' The boy's voice sounded taut.

'First of all, open your hood. Do it now.' Perowne saw the cover slide back. 'Fine. Now I'll tell you the easiest way. Roll over on your back, trim her a bit tail heavy, then yank the harness pin and you'll just fall clear. That's all there is to it.'

'Yessir!'

'Good lad. Now do it.'

The Spitfire suddenly rolled to starboard, twirling the trail of black smoke, and Perowne eased slightly higher and to one side waiting to see the Sergeant drop from the machine.

'I can't do it, sir.' The smoke billowed thicker.

'Of course you can. You've plenty of height. You'll drift down nicely. And we'll stick around to see you picked up.'

'I can't make myself.' At any second the wounded Spitfire would explode. Perowne thought of the twenty-year old boy, sweating with fear and with the sea rushing above his head. 'You can Johnny, and you will.'

'No, sir. I'd rather stay in her.'

'Johnny – she'll explode!!' The Sergeant made no reply, and his aircraft began to dip slightly towards the sea. 'Johnny, can you hear me? We need you, I need you. Remember, only three in the squadron have brought down a Hun – Flight-Lieutenant MacIntyre, me, and you. We can't spare you, Johnny. I'm counting up to four, and on four you'll pull that pin. Here I go. One. Two. Three. Four . . .'

A black shape fell from the Spitfire, twisting and somersaulting until a sudden spurt of white streamed upwards and the parachute opened. Perowne immediately banked to port. Johnny wanted to live because he had killed. The abandoned Spitfire dipped further forwards and dived to meet the water in a gentle angle; the machine hit the surface of the sea with a flat shower of spray, bounced, then tipped and began to sink. Johnny's parachute drifted in steady descent.

Perowne spoke to George, still circling. 'Hello, Orange Two. I'll stay with him as long as the fuel lasts. You make for Lympne – I think that's the nearest coastal airfield. Give the present fix to the naval rescue boys, re-fuel and get back. If I have to leave, I'll take the latest fix with me. Don't radio for help or you may attract the Huns. OK?'

He peered upwards to see George's Spitfire curve north-east, and he resumed his circle round the falling parachute. Almost immediately, Johnny hit the water and the white silk floated down around him. Moments later, a head bobbed up beside the parachute, and Perowne could see the yellow Mae West and a waving arm as he flew low over the pilot. He waggled his Spitfire's wings and climbed to circle again, glancing at his fuel gauge and trying to calculate how long he would be able to stay: twenty-five minutes, perhaps slightly longer if he cut it fine. George should just about make it back in time. Meanwhile, Perowne knew he would be a sitting target for enemy aircraft as he waited alone above the Channel.

They came ten minutes later, six of them high to starboard, flying first in pairs then diving in line astern. For a moment, Perowne believed the approaching aircraft might be Spitfires, until he noted the bent wings and spatted legs of the Ju 87 Stuka. Johnny must have heard their fearful high-pitched screech as they began their descent. Perowne glimpsed again the tiny speck of yellow in the vast sea below him, then he banked towards the enemy.

He had perhaps ten seconds in which he could attempt to save himself by abandoning the pilot. Perhaps rescuers might still be able to find Johnny later – but the speck seemed so minute, and the sea so huge. He thumbed forward the gun catch and prepared to face the diving Stukas.

They came towards him in a steep slant. As they approached, they split, two aiming directly at him, four curving behind, and he knew he stood no chance of survival sandwiched between them. In those last seconds, he realized with surprise that he felt no fear, merely disbelief and a swamping sadness. The two Stukas to his front appeared in the reflector sight – still too far to shoot. He glanced to left and right with a last instinctive struggle for survival, but the other Stukas were sweeping in to block any banking escape. He looked to the front again, and his thumb flexed to push the button.

And then, incredibly, the Stukas banked to port and starboard on either side of him, rolling away to leave him room. He wrenched his head to the left, and saw the Stuka on his beam drawing level with the speed of its dive, and as the aircraft closed he could see the waggling wings. He pushed the stick and rudder into a climbing turn, still uncomprehending, until he looked below and saw the Stukas circling the pilot in the water, and he imagined Johnny's terrible fear turning to relief when he realized that the Germans were sparing their lives. Perhaps, like Johnny, one of them had suffered such a sea ordeal; perhaps a pilot's simple bond united them, until the next encounter. Moments later, Perowne and Johnny were alone again, and the wait for rescue was resumed.

Johnny returned to the airfield late that evening, proud of his experience; he praised the crew of the rescue craft, boasted of his conquest over a young nurse at Folkestone Hospital where he'd gone for a check-up, and he was happy to allow Simon to get him thoroughly drunk. The mess had another reason for celebration: Lex's third kill, this time a Heinkel over France. Simon led the singing with a vigorous version of the current favourite – 'Take the piston rings out of my stomach'.

Perowne, sitting in the corner of the mess with his pint, waited for the telephone to ring. The latest replacement, Sergeant 'Henny' Fowler, had failed to return from the afternoon sortie, although he'd been seen re-crossing the Channel. Joe sat with Perowne, reserved as always.

The telephone rang beside the bar. Henny Fowler had landed in a field near Dover, wounded in the leg and arm and with his aircraft a write-off: Perowne left the mess to write the report, and to search for additional replacements. Joe sat alone in the corner, and the noise at the bar seemed to change into the roar of aircraft engines: he felt himself turning and twisting again as he sought to escape from the Me 109. He'd so nearly died that day. One minute the sky seemed clear, and the next moment, the Huns had dived from the sun, and he'd rolled and dropped and escaped, all in less than five seconds. Any one of those seconds could have been his last. Joe looked up from his drink, and stood to make the effort to join the others.

All available pilots were listed 'on state' next morning, except for Johnny Wright. They gathered at dispersal in the half-light, with the air cold enough to make them shiver in their Irvin flying-suits. An orderly fed the stove, and the pilots sat slumped in the shabby arm-chairs or lolled across the table. Perowne walked imme-diately to the telephone, clicked the receiver arm, and asked for the Met. report. He turned and told the others, 'Ten-tenths cloud over northern France. Fresh north winds bringing clearance by noon. We'll have to wait.'

Slowly, the sun rose above the Downs to wash over the quiet, expectant airfield, and to shorten the shadows beneath the beeches. George played chess with the latest arrival, Sergeant 'Birdie' Dickinson; Lex jumped up every few minutes to pace impatiently, and each time, Simon swore at him for disturbing his peace; Joe tried to read a tattered paperback.

Perowne finished his letter to Anna, and didn't know why: today was their anniversary and he'd be driving the thirty miles to London during the evening. Two sorties – only one, if the weather failed to clear until the afternoon – and the wait would be over. He'd fought so hard against going to see her more often because he feared the contrast between his war and her love, but tonight had been promised.

Joe abandoned his paperback, and went outside to lay in the sun. Mops settled beside him, and he fingered the dog's shaggy hair: she slumped lower, and soon she began to twitch with her dreams. Joe closed his eyes, his face upturned.

The telephone rang, and the pilots shuffled immediately to their feet. Perowne replaced the receiver. 'False alarm. The weather's still down over the Channel.'

The shadows dwindled into deeper purple beneath the six waiting Spitfires. Joe stood and told Mops to stay, and he walked over the grass to check his aircraft, even though he knew he'd no need. His parachute waited on the tail. He climbed up into the cockpit, and ran his hand over the instruments – petrol tanks full, tail trimming wheel neutral, airscrew fine pitch, directional gyro set, gloves ready, helmet on reflector sight with oxygen and R/T leads connected . . . He returned to the waiting Mops, slumped beside the dog, and at last fell asleep.

Then, he wakened with a start. The pilots were rushing from the hut, struggling into Mae Wests, pulling on silk gloves and Irvin jackets. 'Come on, you idle blighter,' shouted Simon, and Joe pulled himself to his feet, called to the orderly to keep hold of Mops, and sprinted after the others, his heart suddenly pounding, his throat dry, and the familiar sickness in his stomach.

CHAPTER FOUR

They crossed the French coast near Fécamp, heading for the battle area east of Rouen. The sky had almost cleared: above the Spitfires, the cover was too thin to be of any help in an attack, and Perowne could see the blue shining through the mist. He looked down at the map on his knee and found the squadron's patrol line – Yvetot to Gournay, then south-east as far as Beauvais. He glanced in his mirror then spoke to Lex, leading the second section.

'Hello, Orange Leader. Loosen the Vic.' He saw the Spitfires to the port and starboard of Lex's machine move apart, carrying out the new tactics which he and his pilots had arranged, and he spoke to his own Numbers Two and Three – Joe and 'Birdie' Dickinson. Ten minutes later, the squadron reached Yvetot and the start of the patrol line, and as the Spitfires flew steadily south-east, Perowne observed the smouldering villages, columns of black smoke and burning copses which indicated the latest German thrust towards Rouen and the Seine. His pilots said nothing, with even Simon quiet, but over the R/T came sounds of dogfights somewhere to the south – calm commands interrupted by curses and shouts and sometimes screams – and Perowne wished the R/T would become silent: the noise of battle would tense the nerves of his own pilots even tighter.

'Bandits. Way out on the port beam.' Joe's voice sounded suddenly near after the distant hubbub on the radio. Perowne could just see the formation flying to the east – most likely bombers with a strong fighter escort. 'Too far into Hun territory,' he said. 'We've to stick to our line.'

They flew above the main Rouen-Abbeville road, and Perowne noted the line of abandoned French trucks. Then they reached Gournay to find the town battered almost to complete rubble. Perowne checked his fuel gauge, examined the map for the location of his specified refuelling airfield on the outskirts of Rouen, and told his pilots, 'Vector Nine-Oh to Station Charlie. We'll stop off for lunch.'

'And about time. My stomach's giving me hell.' Simon had still to restrain his chatter over the R/T. Then two pilots spoke at once, one of them Birdie. 'Hun! Bandits to port! ... Here they come!'

'I see them.' Perowne guessed the Me 109s to be at least a dozen in number, diving in rough pairs. 'Break. Break. Break.' He snatched a glance to either side and in his mirror: the Spitfires were banking to port and starboard, climbing to face the fighters. He pulled back the stick and boosted the throttle, and almost immediately a 109 swung into his sights: he fired, but could see no effects. He half-rolled after another, pressed the button again, then keeping the enemy in his sights, pressed once more; he caught a glimpse of a Spitfire diving to his left, on the tail of a Messerschmitt, and another Hun curving to the south. The enemy in front of him dropped away, and he followed. In his efforts to keep the sights fixed, he forgot the position of his aircraft – whether rolling, upside down, diving, climbing. He fired again and this time, slices of aircraft wing were flung sideways from the 109.

He thrust his aircraft in a sudden half-roll in case a second enemy machine might be on his tail, then he climbed after another, boosting his throttle again, and he continued to fire until his Brownings suddenly ceased to respond and he knew he'd expended his ammunition. He immediately pushed forward the column and dived steeply, levelling out at about 1,000 feet in a gentle slant to about 200 feet, then he headed over the trees towards Rouen, at the same time searching around him for signs of other Spitfires. He flashed low over a farmyard, and caught a glimpse of a woman herding cattle. The houses of Rouen rose in front of him. He banked and found the bomb-cratered airfield. Two Spitfires were down, and another just landing, and Perowne smiled with relief as he noted the numbers – Lex, Simon, Joe. His wheels touched, and he taxied towards the hut in the corner.

An officer ran through the doorway and hurried towards him, shouting up at Perowne even before the pilot had opened the cockpit cover. 'Sorry. You can't stay. I've told the others – we're just off.'

'What the hell for?'

'Huns. They've bombed twice this morning, and will do again at any moment. And German ground units are within six miles. We've nothing left here – no fuel, ammo, nothing.'

Perowne and his pilots found the next airfield on the map – thirty-five miles to the west of Rouen. They waited five minutes for George and Birdie, with Lex explaining in detail the damage he'd inflicted on two 109s – 'one went down for certain'. No more aircraft appeared. Perowne could feel the sweat drying cold between his shoulder-blades; he knocked out his pipe, climbed back into the cockpit which still reeked of cordite, and the four Spitfires took off again. Perowne led the way, keeping low over the fields and hedges and anxiously noting his dropping fuel gauge. He located the improvised airstrip – a cut wheat field – and came in to land, bumping and bouncing over the ruts and finally cutting his engine near the tents beneath the trees. A petrol tanker immediately moved out of the shadow, and men hurried forward to refuel the machines: other fitters swarmed over the wings to feed each Spitfire's eight Brownings with daisy-chain belts of ·303 ammunition. The pilots slumped into the shade, jackets open and parachutes beside them, and they waited again for the missing pair. Perowne checked his watch. In six hours, he would be with Anna.

Lex broke the silence. 'Well, it's not bad so far. How about you Simon – did you get one?'

'Christ knows. I just blasted away.'

Joe spoke, for the first time since Perowne had landed at Rouen. 'It all seemed so chaotic. I can't even remember firing.'

Simon climbed to his feet. 'I'm bloody hungry. I'll see about fodder.' He returned almost immediately to say he had bullied the loan of a car to take them into the nearest village, two miles away, where they could buy food. Perowne felt he should stay at the field in case George and Birdie arrived, but he knew he could do nothing, and the four pilots climbed into the huge, ugly Citroën which Simon had commandeered. Simon drove, rushing down the straight white road at a ridiculous speed, with the poplars flicking past on either side. They drew up in the cobbled square and crowded into the small café, where Simon persuaded the fat madame to accept an English pound note in return for cold meat, tough brown bread and a jug of watery wine. Lex continued to talk of the fighting, with Simon occasionally joining in; Perowne and Joe sat silent for most of the miserable meal. Outside, the square seemed peaceful, except for the frequent despatch riders who roared through, and Perowne could hear the distant guns thudding like summer thunder. He felt hot, sticky and uncomfortable in his fur-lined flying suit and boots.

Thirty minutes later, they were back at the field, to find Birdie sitting beneath the trees. Perowne gave him the cold meat which he'd thought to stuff in his pocket: Birdie had seen George bale out, and with any luck he would be safe.

Perowne sought further orders, crouching over the field telephone in the stuffy tent, while his pilots stripped themselves to the waist and lay in the sun, looking very white and very clean. Through the tent doorway, Perowne could also see French civilians making a haystack in the far corner of the field; closer, a group of loud-talking and cheerful airmen were belting ammunition. At last, the voice crackled over the telephone wire from the local Air Control: the squadron must resume patrol, but with even greater care since the battlefront was shifting towards Rouen at an increasing pace – the original patrol line now lay at least six miles in enemy territory.

The five machines took to the air, and to Perowne, the group seemed very small and vulnerable. They flew above Rouen with Perowne's apprehension steadily resurging as they neared the front. Suddenly, the sky around the Spitfires became littered with black puffs of smoke as German anti-aircraft guns began to fire. Perowne climbed, then dived, then climbed again to avoid the gunners being able to establish the correct height, and the Spitfires reached their turning point west of Beauvais, apparently undamaged. He banked to return northwards, and in front he could see the weird patterns woven by the drifting anti-aircraft smoke, marking the path of his pilots on the southward run. Now they had to return.

But suddenly the puffs ceased to appear. Perowne immediately guessed the reason. 'Get ready. Hun fighters must be on their way. We'll start climbing now.'

Less than fifty seconds later, the German aircraft appeared to the east, flying in layers and seeming like an organized swarm of bees. Perowne continued to lead his squadron upwards – 16, 18, 20,000 feet – until the first layer of enemy moved at a lower level, although the second layer still flew above. Perowne estimated German strength to be at least twenty aircraft, some Dornier bombers which continued to fly west presumably for Rouen. The German fighter escort began to circle, closing steadily for the kill. Two pairs, above the Spitfires, peeled into a dive.

'Break! Break! Break!'

'See you later, boys.'

'Tallyho!'

Perowne singled out a 109 diving to his starboard. He banked, tried to judge deflection, and fired, but the enemy continued to half-roll towards him. He fired again. The two aircraft looped and rolled, and for an instant he exposed his Spitfire's belly to the 109's fire, and his aircraft juddered violently as the cannon shells struck the hull: then with sweat pouring down his face, his arms and legs aching, and a fierce pain thudding at his brain, he twisted further in the roll and the dogfight continued. At last he managed to manoeuvre towards the 109's tail. The German pilot turned on his back attempting a dive but another two-second burst from the Spitfire caught the Hun and the 109 began to blaze. A small shape dropped from the flames, falling faster than the debris: Perowne watched for a moment but the German's parachute failed to open.

He climbed again and managed to latch onto the tail of another 109. He fired twice then suddenly his aircraft lurched again from cannon shells, shaking violently, and a shadow blocked his view as a Me 110 flashed above him; he broke to starboard, somehow found his 109 target still in front of him, and pressed hard on the button. The enemy immediately plunged into a sharp stall turn to port, twisted into a spin, and then struck straight into a Me 110 which had been banking beneath. The two German aircraft seemed to hang motionless then started to fall together in a flaming embrace; Perowne watched appalled – the aircraft broke apart a few hundred feet above the pale green fields and crashed in a burst of purple smoke just a few yards apart. Voices on the R/T chattered into his consciousness.

'Orange Two. I'm on your tail.'

'Good lad, Joe. Here we go!'

'Got the bastard! Christ, how I got him!'

'Watch out behind, Orange One. He's coming in!'

Perowne looked above him but the sky appeared to be empty; his pilots continued to shout into the R/T, perhaps from further to the west, but with his ammunition exhausted, he had to leave them. He checked the ground below with the map and turned for home, flying as low as possible; once he swept over a Panzer column and he could see lines of German infantry moving across nearby fields; smoke rose steadily from the east in alternate pillars of white and black.

At last, he crossed the coast but his anxieties continued – for his pilots, and for himself should he be caught in the open without ammunition. His clothes were clinging to him with sweat, and his feet felt as wet as if his boots were filled with water. The sea below him looked cool and endless, with his Spitfire's shadow accompanying him over the swell. Near the south coast, he saw mist banks in front of him, offering welcome cover for the last few miles; he made his landfall near Hastings, and only a few minutes later circled his airfield and dropped down to land.

No other pilot had arrived. Perowne walked slowly

to the dispersal hut, dropped his equipment on the table, and then stood outside to listen and wait. An orderly brought him a deckchair, into which he sank; Joe's dog, Mops, sat restlessly beside him. The sun felt warm on his stiff face, although the shadows had begun to lengthen again beneath the beeches. Six o'clock. By now he should be getting ready to drive to London. Still he waited.

Mops heard the engines first and began to whine. Perowne sat forward and spotted the moving flecks above the Downs to the south – two aircraft. He searched behind them for a third and fourth but the two were alone. They circled once and came in together: Lex and Birdie. Mops began to bark and Perowne told her to sit. 'Not yet, girl. Not yet.'

Lex had killed again. Birdie claimed his first definite and one probable; neither had seen anything of Simon and Joe, and they sat together outside dispersal to continue the wait.

Joe returned five minutes later. This time Perowne allowed Mops to run to the figure climbing from the cockpit, and the pilot walked towards dispersal with the dog barking and jumping beside him. Joe believed he'd severely damaged a 110, but hadn't been able to see if the aircraft went down; his own machine had a section missing from the tail. Now he lay on the grass, eyes closed, with the dog resting her head on his chest, and Perowne noted the pallor of the boy's face and the fleck of blood where his teeth had dug into his lower lip.

One by one the pilots moved off to the mess, Lex leaving first. Perowne shook Joe gently by the shoulder. 'Go and have a good wash. You'll feel better for it.'

'I'd rather wait for Simon.'

'He won't be coming back here tonight. It's too late.'

'I know. But he'll ring.'

44

'Of course he will. Come on, we'll wait in the mess.'

The telephone in the bar remained silent and the wait began to steal time which Perowne should have spent with Anna. He couldn't leave. He knew he'd feel guilty making love to Anna; he also knew he was being foolish. A message could easily be passed on. And why only Simon, when others had already gone – Dundas, Jones, Marder, Hyde, Grant, George missing somewhere near Rouen? He couldn't tell; but the silent telephone continued to tie him to the squadron mess.

The harsh jangle shattered the silence of the Chelsea flat. Anna suddenly felt sick. Had Teddy been shot down? She forced herself to pick up the receiver, and her relief at hearing her husband's voice momentarily overcame the disappointment at his message. 'Yes, I understand. Of course I do. I may see you later, darling.' She sat on the floor again, her back against the sofa, her head resting sideways on the arm, the position in which she liked to sit against Teddy, while his hands smoothed her hair. The room grew darker and the flat seemed even more unbearably silent.

The gaunt, yellow-faced French officer could speak no English. Nor had he time to understand the gestures. His regiment retreated towards Rouen, out of touch with any surviving units on either flank. Only two BI tanks remained serviceable – magnificent machines with their 75 mm guns, but now useless without ammunition; successive defensive attempts had been swept aside by Stukas and Panzers; his men verged on mutiny. And now this idiotic British pilot blocked the road and shouted nonsensical words at him. The French officer threw out his hands to indicate lack of comprehension.

'Balls,' said Simon in disgust, and clambered over the

protesting officer into the rear of the Renault.

A few minutes after 10 o'clock, the telephone rang in the mess. A harassed flight-lieutenant at Uxbridge passed the information which had come via Le Havre, Portsmouth and London, that Flying Officer Simon Tattersall had reached elements of the British 51st Division and required transport home. 'According to the somewhat garbled message we got, he's creating one hell of a stink. But we've a couple of other pilots in the area so don't worry about it – we'll fetch 'em in a communications plane.'

Five minutes later Perowne was driving to London; Joe settled to sleep, Mops at his feet, and with the empty bed across the room no longer haunting him.

CHAPTER FIVE

Anna felt his sleeping breath against her breast and his thigh heavy across her own, and gently she pulled the sheet higher around them. Teddy murmured, his fingers clutching her stomach, and she thought he must be waking again, then his breathing eased. She felt warm and drowsy and secure for the moment. His shoulders were thin beneath her arm. The clock ticked in the dark room, and her hatred of the sound steadily increased.

'Anna?'

'Yes? I'm awake.'

'I must get back by dawn.'

'I know. There's time yet.'

She sensed his mouth moving into a smile. 'For what?' He stirred from under her arm to reach over, and light burst from the bedside lamp; now he lay across her, looking down into her face, and she traced her fingers lightly across his cheecks and beneath his eyes. 'You look so tired.' He smiled again and said: 'Hardly surprising, after a night like that.'

'Only half a night.'

'Don't blame Simon.'

'I don't. I blame you. You shouldn't care so much.'

'You're as bad as they are. Lex said the other day that I acted like a broody hen. But now I'm here.'

Her hands met behind his neck, pulling his head down; her tongue found his mouth and she felt the weight of his body moving further onto her as she opened her legs and bent her knees to take him into her once more.

She lay looking up at him while he dressed, noticing

again the thinness of his body and the sag of his shoulders. 'You always did look like a scarecrow,' she said, 'but now you're even worse.' He reached down and pulled back the sheet; her legs were still apart, lazy in the aftermath of love-making, and she raised her arms above her head to rest them on the pillow, showing her body to him. He knelt beside the bed and ran his hands down from the angled elbows, softly over her breasts, feeling the tightening of the skin as he passed, and over the flatness of her stomach to the hair below, and down to the wetness between her open thighs. She moved gently against his fingers, her hips rising and falling, and he continued pressing against her and into her until she bent her legs and thrust hard, hips raised from the crumpled sheet, suddenly moaning before she sank back. Her eyes were huge and with almost an expression of fear, they searched his face; then she tightened her thighs to keep him there a moment longer.

'That wasn't fair,' she whispered.

He smoothed her hair from her deep brown eyes. Then he kissed her softly, his lips barely brushing her mouth, and he stood. 'I'll tuck you in and then I must go.'

'I'll get up now.'

'No – you stay. I like you being there. You look as if you're waiting for me.'

Joe stamped hard on the rudder bar and his Spitfire broke abruptly starboard, but the Me 109 was still behind, and tracer flashed red just above his cockpit. He tried for height, hugging the stick, yet the 109 followed him up, and the tracer curled away just beneath the Spitfire's wings. He thrust the stick forward and clutched onto it with all his strength, and his aircraft banked with its nose down; he almost blacked out as he dived, then the horizon screwed violently as he tried to level and turn his aircraft into a half-roll. But the ugly black shape still quivered in his mirror, and flashes burst from its guns. The Spitfire shuddered, and vibration jarred up his legs; he flung her into a vertical dive, his arms aching.

A shell ricocheted off the perspex hood. Others tore into the fuselage and slammed into the plating behind his seat, and as the ground loomed ahead the 109 seemed to be gaining, the French shoreline dithering and wavering below. Joe jerked back the stick in desperation, almost too quickly – the aircraft creaked but began to level, and the 109 had dropped beneath him. The German started to level, but by then Joe was climbing, up towards the sun.

Suddenly the sky was free again. He banked to port still climbing, waggling his wings to watch the blind spots and seeing nothing. For the first time he heard his gasping breath. He altered course to fly across the Channel, alone, with no ammunition and still drenched with fear.

Then the white glycol coolant began streaming from his engine. The cylinder must have been punctured, and already the oil temperature was sliding upwards, with the roar of the engine taking a different note. He throttled back into coarse pitch. For a moment, he thought of turning back towards France, then he remembered the 109s and 110s which had been swarming around Le Havre, attracted to the British evacuation, like wasps round jam, and he continued over the Channel praying his engine would last out. He sat rigid with the control column tight in his hands, his senses taut and his heart throbbing to the thrust of the engine. His eyes continually twisted from the sky to the sea to the dials on the instrument panel. The setting sun speared into his cockpit, and he felt that any moment the Huns would dive from the glare onto his crippled machine. The sea surged below, and he thought of the hours he would suffer, bobbing like a helpless cork in his Mae West until drowning delivered him. Sweat trickled down his cheek, like a scuttling insect.

A thin smudge appeared on the horizon, and gradually the shape took form, focusing into cliffs and fields and woods. He crossed the coast near Newhaven. Now he could escape by parachute, but he stayed with his aircraft, coaxing her on and talking to her while the oil temperature rose steadily higher. He flew low over the slopes of the Weald and into Kent, then, past Tonbridge, the engine started to seize and he knew he must go down. He searched the ground and saw a field, startling green in the evening light, tempting him to land. It lay flat and straight between dark woods and he came in direct with no time for more than one approach, praying the field would be as level as it looked.

Thank God, the undercarriage and flaps still worked. The grass seemed to leap up, the wheels touched and squealed; the Spitfire bucked, bounced again and lurched forward. The starboard wheel snagged, and the aircraft slewed sideways. Joe cracked his head, but touched the right brake and the Spitfire straightened. At last, she stopped. The engine cut, and in the sudden clear silence, voices sounded loud over the R/T from engagements still taking place somewhere in the Channel. Screams and obscenities continued until Joe unplugged the lead from his helmet; he unbuckled his harness, and climbed out to lay on the grass. He sobbed at the touch of the turf beneath his fingers. Then he stood, looked around him, and began to walk.

Susie saw him coming. He'd walked halfway up the

track to the farm when she noticed him. She quickly put down her pail and milk slopped down her skirt, warm on her bare legs. 'Peter,' she called. Her brother grumbled in the cowshed behind her, and she heard him clank down his bucket. She watched the man as he walked slowly up the lane, his flapping flying boots powdered with the dust which silted between the winter ruts, his helmet hanging loose in his hand, and his face white beneath the black of his untidy hair. She felt Peter stand beside her. He stood as still as she for a moment, then ran to the yard gate; he walked quickly along the lane, and the man stopped as he approached. Susie heard their voices, then they came on together.

'His aircraft crashed,' called Peter. 'In the long meadow I think. But he's all right.'

The man stood in front of her. She saw the dirty paleness of his face and the blue of his eyes, and the red trickle on his cheek; he noticed her glance and touched his cheek with the back of his hand.

'It's stopped bleeding,' he smiled. 'I'm sorry if I frighten you.'

'You don't.'

'I'm Joe. Your brother – is he your brother? – was right. I had to come down in the field, and I'd like to use your telephone.'

'Were you fighting?' asked Peter and gave no time for an answer. 'Have you a Spitfire?'

Joe smiled at him, merely nodding in reply; to Susie, he seemed very young and shy. Behind her, she could hear the calves lowing gently for their food. 'Come to the house,' she said, turning to lead the way, and they walked across the yard, with Peter still chattering.

Their mother fussed around Joe, exclaiming at his cut face. 'Put the kettle on girl,' she said, and Susie brought out the cups. The pilot used the telephone in the hall, and they could hear his voice through the open kitchen door. 'No it'll patch up ... yes I think so ... Is Simon back? ... Thank God – give him my love ... And the others? ...'

Susie's mother insisted he sat at the kitchen table while she bathed his cut, and Peter asked one quick question after another. The pilot's answers were friendly enough but without details, and avoiding any description of the fighting in which he had been involved only a few minutes before. Susie sat silent at the other end of the long table and looked at him. The smell of Dettol mingled with her mother's cooking. His dirty yellow Mae West lay across the back of the sofa next to the untidy pile of farming magazines and scattered newspapers; his helmet was hung over a chair. To Susie, the pilot was alien. His words sounded unnatural, even when he spoke ordinary sentences such as his polite praise for the tea and cake. His face appeared even paler beside Peter's sunburn and her mother's flushed cheeks, and his boots were huge and ugly on the rug's faded pattern. Even the dog sensed something strange: she approached slowly to sniff his legs, then slipped back into her box, tail straight, instead of pestering as she usually did with visitors.

An aircraft sounded faint above the farm and Joe suddenly cocked his head, birdlike, to listen. 'Hurricane,' he said, as if to himself. His long fingers played with the handle of the cup, then with the fringe of the cloth. He looked up quickly as Susie stood; she went out to feed the calves, saying nothing, with Nellie padding at her heels.

The animals were gulping greedily from their buckets when Susie's father arrived back from market, his van bumping into the yard. Later, while Susie swilled the flags between the stalls in the quickly fading light, the truck came to take the pilot away. Susie stood in the shadow of the doorway, feeling the warmth from the stones soak into her bare feet, and she watched him walk from the porch; Nellie growled slightly, deep in her throat. Susie heard the pilot's voice. 'Goodnight, Mrs. Barrett and to you, sir. Cheers, Peter – say my thanks to Susie.'

So he knew her name. He looked across the yard towards her, but perhaps couldn't see in the dusk, and the truck drove noisily away. Susie stood while the sound of the engine dwindled down the lane and onto the main Maidstone road, and while the smell of the exhaust was replaced by the scent of the night-stocks in her mother's garden.

Simon, standing beside Perowne at the bar, turned quickly when the mess door opened. He shouted, 'Joe! You little pipsqueak!' He clambered over an armchair, ignoring the indignant protest from Johnny Wright, and flung his arms round his comrade in a whooping bear-hug. 'Where the hell have you been – coming home at this time of night?'

'What about you, you great ape? Larking with those French girls, I suppose. What time did you get back?' Joe retorted.

Perowne sat with his pipe and his drink in the arm-chair by the fire and listened to the chatter. For a moment, he felt reasonably relaxed. Simon had returned during the late afternoon, none the worse for his forced landing near Rouen; Joe seemed fine; Johnny Wright had recovered from his Channel ditching two days ago; Lex was miserable since he'd failed to bring down another Hun during the day, but doubtless he'd recover; three replacements had arrived, Pilot Officer Womack and Sergeants Fisher and Dent. So, with himself and

Birdie Dickinson, the active squadron pilot strength had been brought to nine. Henny Fowler should be returning soon, and one more replacement was promised.

George Barclay was still missing. Now, forty-eight hours after his disappearance east of Rouen, Perowne believed the pilot must be dead or captured. A pity – George had seemed so solid and sensible, a sobering and efficient example for the rest, and something of a balance to Lex's recklessness and Simon's rugger-scrum approach. The newcomer, Alan Womack, appeared to be a similar sort of character to George, although not in looks : he resembled an evangelical preacher, thought Perowne, very tall, gaunt, and bushy-browed. But he seemed to share George's self-containment and subtle strength.

And they'd need all the strength possible. Perowne remembered the latest Fighter Command Intelligence summary, issued that morning and dated the previous evening, 8 June, which forecast increasing Luftwaffe pressure against the crumbling French, obviously prior to a further massive thrust for Paris, combined with pressure on the British 51st Division. The latter seemed in danger of being isolated in the Havre peninsula. Rouen had fallen during the day; increased enemy air activity over England was reported – '168 enemy aircraft were plotted over the UK and along our coasts between 10 pm and 3 am on the night of the 7th.' It seemed as if the holocaust of Dunkirk was only a prelude to even greater turmoil. And already, in the ten days since the squadron's first operational flight, six pilots had been killed or were missing, and only three – Perowne himself, Lex, and Birdie, had so far avoided having to bale out or crash land.

Perowne pulled himself up from his chair and went

to join the others at the bar to stop himself from beginning to brood again. At least, the pilots seemed resilient; now they had started to sing a crude version of 'Don't Go Any Higher Jeremiah', Simon's voice above the others as usual.

Lex lay in his bed in the dark room, and tried to switch his thoughts, but, as always, he failed. At least, he would be 'off state' the next morning, allowing him another twelve hours of survival. The room seemed somehow bigger without Barclay; Lex had told the others that he'd be able to sleep without George's snoring, but in reality, he missed the steady rumble from the other bed. Poor bugger. Lex imagined the body in the Spitfire wreckage, or perhaps just charred remains amidst an indefinable molten mess. Lex dragged hard at his cigarette, and the sudden red glow reflected in the mirror on the far wall. It could be his turn tomorrow.

At least, he was fooling the others, even Teddy, and not much escaped the CO's careful, conscientious scrutiny. Lex had seen Perowne examining them, one by one, and the pretence seemed harder at such times. He envied them all, especially Simon. Christ, he was always so cheerful and certain. Lex felt slightly safer when Simon flew as his Number Two to guard his tail – yet at the same time the desire to impress Simon, above all the rest, drove him even harder. It had been the same when he'd gone climbing in New Zealand – always wanting to push ahead to hide his terror, to lead rather than being roped second, because in that way no-one would see the expression on his face, and always with the picture of his body at the foot of the crags and the sight of himself in death. And on his father's sheepfarm, he always felt the need to ride the wildest horse in front of the hands; then, at Cambridge, he gained a reputation as an evasive fly-half, but his skill had only come through his fear of being thrown and trampled upon by the opposing forwards.

So, instead of being a coward, he was becoming an 'ace' – four for certain, perhaps five, and another probable. Christ, he'd show them. His cigarette glowed again on his pale, slightly freckled face and on the ginger of his hair. Yet each kill did nothing to diminish his fear; instead he watched his victims spiralling down in flames, wingless, in pieces, and he imagined them to be him.

Joe returned to the farm, soon after the morning's milking. The blue-grey truck drove up the lane, and Susie watched from the kitchen sink as an airman jumped down to open the gate. The vehicle pulled up before the porch, and Susie wiped her hands then met the pilot on the step.

'We've come to see to my aircraft.' His hair was tidier now with the black curls brushed down, but his face still looked pale, and Susie noticed the deepening bruise around the cut on his cheek-bone.

'Can we get the truck down to it?'

'If you go through the orchard.' Susie hesitated then added: 'Should I come to show you?'

He smiled. 'Please.'

The truck bounced down the lane, and she directed the driver into the apple orchard; white blossom fluttered down as the vehicle brushed the trees. 'There she is,' said the pilot, and Susie saw the Spitfire for the first time. She expected it to be far more damaged, but instead it sat in the open between the beech trees, nose pointing proudly upwards and wings low, crouched as if ready to spring back into the air; the engine seemed large and long, and the cockpit small.

Peter ran forward as the truck stopped. 'Isn't she

beautiful? I've been having a look at it. Can I help to mend it?'

The pilot smiled as he helped Susie down. She walked behind them to the Spitfire, and she ran her hand along the smooth wing then saw the black smudge on her fingers. 'From the guns,' said the mechanic. Susie quickly wiped her hand on her skirt; she noticed the ripped fabric and the neatly spaced holes along the aircraft's flank which stopped only a foot or so from the cockpit, and she turned and walked away. She sat on a bank while Peter chattered, and the men worked on the aircraft engine.

The Spitfire, like the pilot in the farmhouse kitchen the previous evening, seemed out of place in the meadow, an unwelcome intrusion, and Susie hoped the men would soon be finished, and the meadow be clear again. She lay back and felt the sun on her face and on her bare legs. The sky was cloudless; behind her, she could hear a blackbird in the beeches, the cough of a pheasant and flies buzzing in nearby shade. Amongst these tuneless sounds, the metallic clank as the mechanic mended the engine scraped unnaturally harsh.

'She'll soon be fixed.' The pilot sat beside her. 'Then we'll leave you in peace.' Susie sat up quickly and glanced at him. He was staring at his aircraft, where the sun glittered on the perspex hood and the faint breeze fluttered the torn fabric. He said, 'Peter's right you know – she is beautiful.'

He looked unrecognizable in the high cockpit, and the sudden engine roar made Susie put her hands to her ears and turn away. She saw a rabbit scuttle into the undergrowth. Behind her, the roar moved, becoming even louder. Peter stood next to her, facing the aircraft. She felt the ground shudder beneath her bare feet; her skirt tugged against the back of her thighs, and her long

57

hair flew about her head. The grass ceased to flutter, her dress dropped, suddenly still, and she turned to see the Spitfire clearing the trees at the far end of the meadow, banking to come back again, with the sun still glistening on the cockpit hood.

'Marvellous!' shouted Peter. 'Look Susie!' The Spitfire flew lower; when it came above them, Susie noticed the wings dipping and rising in a gesture of goodbye, and, before the machine disappeared above the trees, the aircraft's shadow fell cold across Susie's face. The stench of aircraft fuel lay heavy over the meadow, and a black smear of oil stained the flattened grass.

Joe glanced back at the meadow, then settled down to enjoy the flight home. The controls felt good again, the needles steady on the instrument panel, and he smiled with relief that his Spitfire was fit once more, knowing his nerves would be even more ragged if he had to fly a strange machine. His thoughts returned to the farm and to the family; the mother with her warmth and fuss, the old man sucking his pipe as if it were the most important thing in the world – that, and the apple crop. The boy, so bloody eager – a good kid. How old? About seventeen, Joe supposed – four years younger than himself, but the difference seemed so much greater. And the girl. Joe wondered if they were twins – the same fair hair, big brown eyes, and slenderness. He'd felt so dirty and clumsy beside her, awkward with her silence.

What a difference to the atmosphere at the squadron: the smell of sweat, and stale smoke and beer, oil, and always the talk of war. And how he hated his room, with only Simon's presence to make it bearable. Cold walls, damp to the touch. Scratched lockers and dirty small window with its metal frame bleeding with rust from the condensation. The view outside of the empty airfield with the constant reminder that within a few hours he might take off and not come back, or even worse, might come back with his Spit wounded, unable to land except in a mangled heap. He tried to tug his mind away. He'd decided he'd return to the farm to thank them, knowing at the same time that he would be a fool to go, since the difference between the farm and the squadron only served to make his survival seem more hopeless.

George Barclay sat rigid against the gunner beside him in the back of the truck as the vehicle swayed and bounced over the rubble. He could see the gun on the ammunition trailer in front of him swinging like a huge ungainly pendulum, and it seemed impossible that the weapon would remain on the hook. The noise of the labouring engines smothered the screech of the Stukas as they dropped onto the French village, but he caught the stench of bomb fumes and burning wood as the convoy careered onwards; he saw British and French corpses sprawled on the road, and groups of soldiers huddled against walls and in doorways, and occasionally a crouching figure darted from one burning building to another. A bomb suddenly erupted in front of them, and a house wall teetered and began to slide into the street; he gripped the stanchion tighter as the driver maintained his speed to fling the lorry into the swirling dust. The vehicle bounced off the ground, slewed with the driver desperately twisting the wheel, and then he caught sight of green fields at the far end of the smoking houses.

Ahead lay Le Havre. Behind, less than three miles away, filtered the German advance. The gunner next to George suddenly lurched harder against the pilot's shoulder; George tried to steady him, then pulled his hand away again and noted the stickiness of his fingers;

he glanced to see that the man's face had been half blown away. Carefully, he wiped his bloody hand on the dead gunner's trousers before propping the corpse more securely against the side of the truck. He waited for the next bombs to fall, and glanced dispassionately at the young gunner who sat opposite to him, whimpering. He could do nothing. Soon it would end, one way or the other, and meanwhile he would simply wait.

CHAPTER SIX

Four thousand feet below the aircraft stretched rolling banks of fog, making it impossible to judge where sea ended and land began. Further to the south, the mist lay thinner over the high ground, and isolated hillocks and woods appeared through the blanket, reminding Perowne of a Japanese painting. Beneath that blanket struggled the remnants of the British 51st Division, retreating towards Le Havre; Perowne knew he could do nothing for them, but at least the murk would keep the Stukas away.

He led the six aircraft in a zigzag climb to 12,000 feet with the sun shining in his eyes, then banked to keep the sun behind, and the Spitfires waited. The aircraft circled slowly for five minutes, maintaining the two V-sections – Perowne, Joe and Womack in the first; Lex, Fisher and Birdie in the second.

A black cross moved below them, approaching from the south and silhouetted against the opaque fog. Perowne squinted his eyes to attempt an identification and recognized the blunt, bulbous nose of the Ju-88 bomber – shorter and more compact than the Dornier. He spoke to Lex. 'Bandit. Course Nine-Zero. Junkers.'

'I see him, Piper Leader.'

'Probably reconnaissance.'

'Let me get him.'

Perowne glanced around him. The sky seemed clear. 'OK, Lex. Take your section down. We'll cover.'

By now, the cross had moved to a point almost directly beneath the Spitfires as they hovered, hidden in the sun: the bomber should be an easy victim. Perowne watched Lex's machine twist to port with Fisher then Birdie following in line astern at a near vertical angle, speed rapidly increasing, dropping like kestrels for the kill. The leading Spitfire began to level slightly, coming in from the enemy's rear, and Perowne could hear Lex's excited voice. 'OK, Yellow Section. I'm going in for the first pass. Follow me, Yellow Two.'

'Roger, Yellow One.'

'Here we go!'

Perowne could see Lex's Spitfire approaching the enemy from the most vulnerable point – behind and slightly below – and he could imagine the gunners in the rear and base of the German cockpit trying frantically to swivel their 7·92 mm machine-guns in the direction of the approaching Spitfires. The Junkers began to weave, but by now, Lex had closed the gap. White smoke suddenly puffed from the bomber's fuselage, swiftly turning to black with an orange heart.

'I got him! Christ, boys did you see that! I got the bugger!'

The leading Spitfire looped upwards above the crippled bomber, then twisted into a half-roll and suddenly dived again. Perowne frowned in anxiety: Lex was flying too close to his Number Two, now closing fast for his attack. He heard Lex shout over the R/T, 'Clear off Fisher! He's mine!'

For a second Perowne thought the two Spitfires must surely collide – from his viewpoint high above they seemed to overlap, and he expected to see them plunge together. He heard an unintelligible oath, then the two aircraft sped apart to bank in opposite directions. The bomber had disappeared: it must have dived into the cloud a thousand feet below, seeking safety like a pigeon fluttering into the cover of trees.

'The bastard's gone. And I'd got him. I'd got him. You saw it.'

Perowne tried to keep the anger out of his voice. 'OK, Yellow Section. We'll join again.' He glanced at his watch: 2.30 p.m. 'We'd better make for home.' The aircraft linked in two V-sections once more, and headed over the fog towards the Channel.

Land breezes pushed the fog north-east during the evening, exposing Le Havre, and the Stukas gathered above the unprotected British troops. George sat with the gunners in a dry ditch beside the bomb-cratered road; he pulled the map from his flying-suit pocket, smoothed out the creases, and found their approximate position – the road led directly to Le Havre, three miles away. Above him, on the verge, stood the gunners' lorry, now without fuel; similar useless vehicles were abandoned nearby. Files of troops tramped wearily towards the coast, and George could hear the chatter of machine-gun fire from across the fields behind him, interspaced with the hollow crump of mortars.

A Bofors began to bark in the distance. Almost simultaneously, he detected the drone of aircraft engines approaching from the south. Another Bofors joined the steady, pumping beat of the first; he eased himself round in the ditch, shaded his eyes with his hand, and caught the glint of the sinking sun on aircraft fuselages. He spoke calmly to the young gunner captain who had been attempting to brew tea on a portable petrol cooker. 'Someone ought to tell those pom-poms to belt up. The range is much too big for them.' The Captain was already looking upwards: sure enough, the small cotton-wool clouds were bursting far below their swift-moving target. The German aircraft took clearer shape, perhaps a dozen, flying in wedge formation, and the drone became a roar. 'Stukas again,' said George quietly.

Suddenly the tip of the aircraft arrow-head broke away, and the roar swelled into a scream. Men on the road began to shout; more Bofors began their panicked coughing, rapidly smothered by the crescendo of noise as the dive-bombers swooped in, straggling line-astern. A gunner near George clutched his hands to his ears then fell in foetal position. The screech became a banshee howl; two soldiers dived for cover in the ditch, one of them clattering over the petrol-cooker and sprawling across George's legs. George sat motionless, watching the man's heaving back as the unearthly sound shredded the sky.

The first bomb burst over to the right, and a man in the ditch clawed violently into the bank as he tried to find greater protection. Only George remained immobile. He saw the vomiting earth as the second bomb dropped closer, and the remains of an exploding vehicle curling slowly high in the air; he saw the way one Stuka dived almost on top of another, each angling upwards immediately after releasing its load, and he noted carefully that now would be the time to attack, when the Hun tried for height again, its belly exposed, its pilot exultant with the death and destruction he'd inflicted below.

Two bombs dropped a few yards down the road, with the thunder of them so close together that they seemed one gigantic explosion, and the earth shook. Dirty yellow and grey smoke rushed up and George observed two men emerging from the dust: each staggered a few paces then crumpled. Another bomb hit the field, and soil showered over the ditch, splattering his dirty blond hair and the back of the man still stretched across his legs. He noticed a worm already crawling

64

from a clump of earth, swinging down onto the soldier's battledress.

The sound of the Stukas dwindled in his ringing ears. He moved his cramped feet and the soldier stirred. 'It's over,' said the pilot. The young captain, on the far side of the ditch, took his hands from his waxen face and kicked viciously at the over-turned petrol cooker. On all sides, soldiers were climbing unsteadily to their feet, and George stood with them. They began to walk towards Le Havre. Only a few yards down the rutted road were spread the remains of two, perhaps three, Stuka victims: two more soldiers knelt beside a comrade who lay with his head back and his breath bubbling through a fearful hole in his throat.

One of the crouching men looked up as George came near, his eyes wild with terror and pain. 'You fucking pilots!' he shouted. 'What the hell are you doing to help? Fuck you! Oh God, fuck you!' His head dropped as he wept into his bloody hands, while George walked steadily on.

Peter spoke from up the ladder. 'I wonder if he'll come again.'

'Who?'

'Joe, of course. And I wonder if he got a Hun today?'

The twins were working in the top orchard, and the evening sky through the apple-branches stretched duck-egg green to a rose horizon. The next day promised to be warm. Susie stopped for a moment to watch the swallows darting backwards and forwards across the field below the house.

She didn't want the pilot to come back. So far, the war had meant so little to her. Even when they'd listened to the Prime Minister announcing that hostilities had begun, the words were unreal and artificial, and the war's early days brought immediate anti-climax, with life on the farm continuing unchanged. The apple-picking, started before the declaration of conflict, went on without interruption; the crates were carefully packed and sent to Maidstone market, and their safe delivery was more important than events across the Channel. Susie had felt no fear, no involvement, and the lack of contact continued throughout the winter and into spring. Even the incredible German advance into Belgium and then France had failed to shake the smooth rhythm of her life: May was the time for preparing the ground in the orchard and checking the trees for sawfly, and all this seemed far more immediate.

Then came Dunkirk. Only a few days ago Susie had seen troops in Maidstone just returned from the French beaches: they were hurried through the town in packed lorries and buses with everyone cheering them. She felt no apprehension, and her detachment remained: those untidy men in motley scraps of uniform bore no resemblance to an army, and she therefore found it impossible to believe that Britain's survival rested upon men such as these. The daily news seemed to have no connection with her daily life. She could not even conceive that Britain needed to be saved. Now the pilot threatened to shatter her peaceful indifference.

They returned to the farmhouse. Susie's father sat by the wireless listening to the news. '. . . Embarkation at Le Havre continues in an orderly fashion. Fog is hindering operations further along the coast at St. Valery, but enemy attempts to isolate the withdrawal are being frustrated. Our aircraft have flown continuous sorties over France during the day, inflicting heavy losses. Five of our pilots are reported missing . . .'

The next morning over 8,000 British troops were forced

to surrender at St. Valery, after the fog had continued to hamper Royal Navy rescue attempts. Perowne sat in his office, studying latest intelligence reports: withdrawal would continue at Le Havre, and orders were to provide maximum air support. Lex should be returning soon from a sortie with six Spitfires across the Channel; Perowne cursed the dwindling French facilities which cut down opportunities for refuelling, so reducing time available over the operational area and increasing the dangers of miscalculation. He only hoped that Lex would curb his enthusiasm.

He sat back and looked through the open window: he didn't know which he found worst, waiting to fly himself or waiting for his pilots to return. He could see the next sortie outside dispersal. Joe stood to one side, playing with his dog. Joe was always so darned reserved, he thought, only really coming to life when he fussed over Mops or fooled with Simon – or when he flew his Spitfire. He handled his machine perhaps better than any of the rest. But he never gave much of himself away, only with his expressive eyes.

The Squadron Leader sighed and turned back to his papers. Four nights since he left Anna; three more to the time when he'd promised to go home again.

Ten minutes later, he threw down his pencil and hurried outside. The sound of the approaching Spitfire grew louder, and a few seconds later he could see it skimming the trees to the south. He glimpsed the number, and the aircraft began to slip sideways in the sign to rearm. Unnoticed, another machine had arrived from the east. Simon. Both banked to land, with Lex leading.

One by one, the aircraft came home, with Perowne anxiously counting the arrival until all six had landed and the pilots were clustered round dispersal, their faces and hair still wet, their cheeks smudged, their eyes still bright with excitement and relief at their safe return. Lex and Simon were arguing over who should claim credit for a downed Me 110, until Simon suddenly slapped Lex on the back and laughed. 'OK, Deadeye. I'll give her to you. But you can buy me a beer.'

Womack had made his first kill; Fisher believed he could claim a probable. Lex reported gathering cloud over Le Havre, which might hinder further sorties in support of the evacuation. The cloud thickened during the afternoon, and the second squadron patrol returned with no contact made; the four aircraft approached the airfield still in neat formation, then split, with Johnny Wright leading the way down. Joe positioned himself last, and for a few minutes he had the sky to himself.

He soared upwards, exhilarated at the freedom and relief from tension, climbing to 12,000 feet and enjoying his solitude without thought for the scolding he would probably receive from Perowne for his skylarking. His Spitfire flew exactly as he wanted her to, responding to the slightest touch and seeming to know his next move before he did. They rolled and half-rolled and looped, and the evening sun above the clouds beamed into the cockpit to turn the wood and metal to gold, and the sky seemed so blue that he felt he could reach out and take a handful home with him. He wanted to fly forever, higher and higher into the sun, and he imagined his Spitfire wanted to take him. Up and up they climbed, then surged into a massive loop onto their backs, before starting to flutter down like a leaf from heaven, shining silver in the sun and swinging backwards and forwards, gently to and fro, and Joe let her take him down to touch the grass.

Showers of spray burst from the night, and over the

bows of the small boat as she tugged at her moorings in the harbour. George had noted the vessel's name as he'd climbed aboard at Le Havre thirty minutes before – *Lucy Jane*. She was a coastal trader, wide across the beam, low in the water but with high gunwales that offered some weather protection. Rain drenched the troops in a steadily increasing deluge, and George bent his head back to lick the moisture running onto his lips. The boat heaved against the swell, straining at the sea anchor then surging back to allow the chain to slap the hull with a dull thud.

The sky glowed to the south, and frequent explosions could be heard over the sound of the waves; each time, huge sparks rose slowly into the lowering night sky. Machine-guns still clattered, and George could see the flecks of tracer from the Brens as the rearguard held off the encircling Germans. Seawards, the night dropped close in a thick and solid blanket, seemingly impenetrable yet offering the hope of safety from the hell which lay over the land; the small boat seemed suspended in limbo between dark and infernal light, between deliverance and destruction.

The decks were slimy with oil, and around George were heaped bloodstained bandages and field dressings and tattered clothing. Nearby, a medical team worked beneath a tarpaulin, struggling to perform emergency operations. Most of the men closest to George seemed asleep, black shapes huddled together and rolling like logs with the boat. He had separated from the gunners during the evening, believing he could move more freely on his own. He doubted if the young captain and his men had even noticed his departure.

The boat throbbed once then stopped then beat again, and the pulse of the engine became steadily quicker. A voice shouted in the dark and the chain rattled; the boat swung free, and spray surged stronger over the bows as she made for the open sea. George began to calculate methodically how long it would take him to cross the Channel, allowing for estimated winds and tide, and thereafter to reach the airfield and his squadron. He supposed he could have tried to contact the squadron from Le Havre, to notify Perowne of his presence, but he had no real purpose. Within twenty hours, his patient wait might be over; he allowed a slight smile of satisfaction, pulled the collar of his Irvin jacket tighter round his neck, and settled down to ignore the elements and to sleep.

CHAPTER SEVEN

George Barclay paid off his taxi and walked into the squadron mess soon after 6 o'clock the following evening, just under twenty hours since leaving Le Havre, including time spent obtaining fresh clothes from his Brighton home. During the day, orders reaching the squadron had specified that operations at Le Havre had ended, with the last troops evacuated before noon. Missions would now be concentrated in the Cherbourg area where British units were still arriving to help the French – despite the imminent German capture of Paris. Two sorties had been undertaken by the squadron – Simon claimed a 109 destroyed – but bad weather during the morning had restricted activity.

All the pilots were in the mess when George appeared, except Lex who had disappeared off to Town. He smiled patiently during the hubbub, nursing his own drink and declining quietly when Simon urged him to have another. He assured Perowne that he would be perfectly fit to fly again the following morning, and began to discuss tactics against Stukas, ignoring Simon's noisy attempts to interrupt.

Henny Fowler came back the next morning, limping and his right arm still in a sling from wounds suffered during his first engagement on 7 June, but insisting vehemently that he'd be 'on state' within two days. An hour later, news reached the squadron that Paris had fallen. Perowne was informed when he returned from another sortie over the Cherbourg peninsula; he immediately remembered the three days spent with Anna in the French capital almost a year earlier – their 'dirty week-end' she'd called it, and he knew she'd be feeling as dismal as he. For a moment he was tempted to telephone her, but instead he forced himself to complete the daily paperwork which he disliked so much.

Three more Germans were shot down for certain by the squadron that day – by 'Birdie', Simon and Womack. All his pilots had returned safely, although Joe had suffered heavy machine-gun fire, and Perowne had noticed that he seemed even paler than usual after the return. He decided to place the boy 'off state' for the following day. He couldn't spare any of the others. Yet the battle over France seemed so useless, since any fool could see the French were beaten. The squadron would do better getting ready for the next stage.

Sitting on his bed with his official documents on his bent knees, he considered for the first time what this next stage might be. Already, Luftwaffe activity over southern England was increasing. He sifted through his papers, and found the latest Fighter Command Intelligence Summary, dated that day, 14 June. 'Between 30–40 enemy aircraft were believed to have been over this country during the night of 12–13 June. 15 fighter patrols were despatched but were unable to intercept. It is considered that these E/A were undertaking reconnaissance missions prior to intensified bombing raids.' A footnote declared that previous instructions not to evacuate further children from cities had been reversed.

Reaching for his pipe he remembered the nursing which Anna had insisted on taking up. He'd treated the idea as a joke; now he recalled the smoking French villages and towns over which he'd flown; he imagined Anna in the midst of similar destruction, and his fingers felt suddenly cold around the warm bowl of his pipe.

Joe drove up to the farm soon after the night dew had dried. He climbed, smiling, out of a battered open car. 'I borrowed it from my room-mate, Simon,' he explained to Peter. 'She's called Felicity after some long-gone girl-friend. And this is Mops.' The huge puppy bounced over from the back seat and out of the door, shaggy hair flopping over its eyes, and tongue lolling. 'I hope Nellie won't mind,' he went on, 'but she could do with a day in the fresh air – like me.'

Susie knelt beside the dog as its long tail scythed backwards and forwards over the cobbles. 'She's lovely.' Then she looked up at the pilot. 'Can you stay for the day?'

'If you'll have me. But I must work for my lunch – what can I do?'

So, he helped them in the orchard, and his shyness slowly melted. Peter delighted in his company as they worked together, driving in stakes for props to support apple branches which would soon be burdened with fruit: they took it in turn to wield the mallet with the other holding the stake, and the sun penetrated the haze which spread over the Downs from the south. The air became steadily hotter and heavier; Peter stripped off his shirt, and soon Joe did the same; Susie, up a ladder to check branches for signs of disease, looked down at them – Peter's back, already as brown as dry bark, his strong shoulders moving easily as he swung the mallet, Joe's thin white arms as he held the stake. Their laughter reached her through the foliage. Joe seemed to be one of them now, and Susie enjoyed his presence, and yet her pleasure was reluctant, since she knew that soon he would be flying and killing again; an alien, moving from one world into another, but this time taking a small part of her with him.

Joe worked throughout the afternoon, and stayed for

supper. By evening, the air seemed heavier than ever, and thunderclouds covered the sunset. Susie, sitting on the porch between Peter and Joe, could sense the pilot's reluctance to leave.

Perowne danced with his wife in the Dean Street night-club, and as his hands tightened around her back he could feel the warmth of her skin through the cotton of her dress. Her hair smelt fresh and clean against his cheek, and he moved his mouth down to the curve of her neck, and immediately her body tensed against him.

Other couples crowded around them, the majority of men in uniform, and through the blue cigarette haze, the small ill-lit room seemed to swirl with greys and browns, filled with a babble of voices and high-pitched laughter driven to rising intensity by the pulsating beat of the band. Anna suddenly took her husband's hand and led him through the dancers to their table, where she began to collect their belongings. 'Let's go,' she said. 'I want you alone again.'

They walked hand in hand through Soho and down Shaftesbury Avenue to blacked-out Piccadilly. Other couples brushed against them on the pavement, some strolling with arms around each other, some hurrying as if anxious to be off the streets. The night air seemed tense. As they entered Lower Regent Street, rain began to fall, and they sheltered for a moment in a doorway before walking on regardless; the wet grass and leaves of St. James's Park smelt sweetly fresh.

Back at their flat, Perowne switched on the radio, then helped Anna to dry her hair. Naked to the waist, she sat between his knees, her arms resting on his thighs and her head bent forward. Suddenly the music ended. The announcer apologised for the interruption, then declared sombrely, 'We have just heard that the French leader Paul Reynaud resigned earlier this evening. The French radio said a few moments ago that Marshal Pétain has been asked to form a new administration. It is understood that Monsieur Reynaud felt unable to continue in view of the serious military situation in his country.'

Perowne's hands still held the towel, but now they rested on Anna's shoulders. To him, the implications of the French political upheaval seemed obvious: the path was being prepared for a French capitulation, and Britain would soon stand alone. Slowly he began to smoothe his wife's hair again.

The squadron flew a last mission over France next morning to cover the evacuation of remaining British troops from Cherbourg. The sky stretched clear over the Channel, and the aircraft approached the French coast at a height of 14,000 feet, with the land curving brown and faded green to a hazy horizon. Perowne made landfall just west of Cherbourg, and all the nine aircraft immediately began to shake their wings as the pilots attempted to locate enemy fighters. Behind Perowne's section flew the second, led by Lex, with Simon's trio in the rear; below lay the familiar scenes of British withdrawal. Dunkirk, Le Havre, now Cherbourg, but now there could be no others.

For ten minutes, the squadron patrolled above the coast, drifting up and down the sky with no sign of the enemy. Then one of the pilots spoke rapidly over the R/T. 'Hello, Piper Leader. Hello, Piper Leader. Bandits, bandits to port.'

Perowne immediately located the thin slanting black line and turned the aircraft, at the same time carrying out the essential preliminaries to battle which had now become routine – switching the gun button to 'Fire', checking his reflector sight, examining the instruments, glancing in the mirror and to right and left – and meanwhile the distance separating the opposing groups closed suddenly, with only a few seconds seeming to pass between the initial sighting and the moment when the German aircraft began to dither in the Spitfire's sights.

Perowne led his section in a beam attack on the leading enemy aircraft – four Heinkel bombers. As usual, he felt calm, reacting mechanically, with thoughts of the task in hand allowing no time for his own fear. His first burst flashed away; he banked to keep the target in his sights and fired again, and his intense concentration partly blocked the voices coming over the R/T.

'Tallyho, Yellow Section!'

'I'm covering you, Lex.'

'Here we go!'

And then George's quiet, deliberate warning: 'All Piper aircraft. All Piper aircraft. Beware bandit fighters. They're coming down on us.'

Simon responded immediately, his voice buoyant. 'Attaboy, George! OK, Blue Section. Let's go to meet them.'

Joe saw Simon's section curve up towards the approaching fighters. In front of him, Joe could see Lex plunging on into the bombers, despite the new threat from the 109s above; the section leader swooped on one Heinkel, tore chunks from its port wing with his first burst, then banked to pursue another. Joe flung his Spitfire to port in the attempt to continue guarding Lex's tail. He whispered to himself, 'Christ, Christ, why doesn't he pull away – he's got one – pull away, Lex. Please pull away.' Two yellow Me 109s hurtled past beneath him, and he instinctively flinched and pressed his thumb on the button, before banking still tighter to follow Lex. The section leader was diving now, almost directly onto a Heinkel, and as Joe fell after him, the German bomber exploded in a boiling mass. The black smoke seemed to Joe like an ugly hole in the sky, into which Lex disappeared. Joe followed regardless. Debris flew around his head, then suddenly the sky was clean again; he saw Lex levelling in front of him, and he boosted his own throttle to keep up. A 109 dived into his vision from the left, apparently aiming for Lex, and he twisted to intercept, firing at the same time, even though he knew the range to be excessive, and his words sounded almost pleading as he shouted over the R/T, 'Lex – behind you! For God's sake, behind you!'

Lex saw the shape hovering in his mirror and for a second, sat frozen with fear. The 109 wavered, rising and falling as it closed, and still Lex could do nothing, then suddenly he clutched back the stick, and his Spitfire began to climb. His eyes still on the mirror, he saw the 109 climbing with him; he felt his aircraft judder, and his terror pushed bile into his throat; the two aircraft seemed linked by an invisible thread.

Joe climbed at the same moment as Lex and the enemy, and his shorter turn closed the gap between them. He fired again, his teeth clenched tight, his forearms quivering from his tensed muscles, and, at last, the 109 broke away. He made no attempt to pursue, instead following Lex's Spitfire as it continued to climb towards the sun. He spoke. 'Hello, Orange Leader. Lex, I think I'm almost out of ammunition. And the fuel looks tricky.' He waited for acknowledgement, and was about to repeat his words when Lex replied, 'OK, Orange Two. We'll go home.' The leading aircraft banked towards the sea and crossed the coast three minutes later; Joe drew almost level, and could see Lex looking towards him. 'Thanks, Joe. Fine flying.' The two Spitfires headed over the Channel at 10,000 feet, fear at last ebbing away.

About ten miles to the east, Perowne likewise set course for home. Beneath him, he could see smoke spiralling from his second victim; weariness surged over him as he looked for other aircraft.

'Hello, Piper Leader. I'm above you and coming down to join. Jesus, what a scrap.'

Perowne smiled at the sound of Simon's voice. 'Hello, Blue Leader. How about the others?'

'God only knows. I saw George chasing a Hun. And one Spit seemed to be on fire.'

Perowne and Simon landed to find George, Lex and Joe already at the airfield waiting outside dispersal. George had seen Birdie Dickinson's aircraft falling in flames, and no parachute had appeared. Johnny Wright arrived five minutes later, and reported seeing Fisher's aircraft plunge into the sea out from Cherbourg. George, Simon and Lex claimed an enemy aircraft each for certain, making five with Perowne's victims; Simon and Lex also recorded probables.

Only an hour later, news reached the squadron that the Pétain Government had asked for an armistice, and French forces were ceasing to fight. Perowne led a second sortie during the afternoon, this time patrolling the Channel without incident. The weather closed down during the night, with blustery winds still sweeping across the airfield at dawn. Two more Channel patrols were undertaken despite the weather; Lex inflicted damage on a reconnaissance aircraft, and Simon attacked two 109s which escaped into cloud; Henny Fowler went back 'on state'.

That evening, the pilots clustered round the wireless

in the mess to hear the report of Churchill's speech to the Commons earlier in the afternoon. Joe stood with his elbows on the bar, his back to the wireless set, and as he listened to the announcer's words, his stomach felt cold with a tension similar to the shivery sensation before school exams; even Simon sat serious-faced in his chair. 'The Prime Minister warned the Commons that the Battle of France was over, and he expected that the Battle of Britain was about to begin. Mr. Churchill continued, "Let us therefore brace ourselves to our duties and so bear ourselves that, if the British Empire and its Commonwealth last for a thousand years, men will still say that this was their finest hour." '

Perowne sat apart while the chatter resumed at the bar, and his mind flitted over the figures which he knew so well, despite the constant additions and subtractions: at the moment, the squadron comprised only nine pilots; nine pilots had been lost since 1 June – an average of one every two days, and ten aircraft. So far, replacements of both men and machines had been satisfactory. But now the 'Battle of Britain' would begin, with even added pressure, and he realized that few, if any, of the pilots in the bar would live to see victory. He glanced round the room. Simon would stand the strain, with his buoyancy carrying him through until a second's error killed him; George had similar strength, in his case obtained through cold calculation – yet even the most brilliant efficiency could not protect a pilot in a dogfight turmoil; Lex would survive until his recklessness took him too far. Perowne's eye's moved to Joe, standing quietly at the edge of the group by the bar – perhaps his superb flying skill would continue to protect him for a few more days. Near to Joe stood Womack, tall and dark and with a secrecy resembling that of George, yet with an added brooding attitude which Perowne felt unable to pierce. And the others? Henny Fowler had recovered well from his wounds, and seemed none the worse for them, and the same applied to Johnny Wright after his Channel ordeal. Sergeant Dent seemed unimaginative and competent, possibly the best qualities to help him survive.

And himself? Perowne shrugged aside consideration of whether he would survive. He just did not know, and, except when he thought of Anna, the question seemed irrelevant. Now the war would come to England, and closer to her, with no defence except the Channel and pilots like his own. We need time, he thought, time to prepare and train, and to become accustomed to the almost incredible realization that those dogfights swirling and twisting over Belgium and France would soon be repeated in the sky above Kent and Sussex, and perhaps even London.

CHAPTER EIGHT

Perowne's prayer for time in which to prepare appeared to be partly granted. A lull fell over the squadron's operational activities after the defeat of France; two sorties were flown each day, but with an average of only six aircraft and with only minimum enemy contact. Simon shot down a Junkers 88 off Dungeness on 21 June; Perowne, Lex and Joe severely damaged a Dornier the following day, although the bomber slipped away into cloud. Two replacements arrived, the gangly, soft-spoken Pilot Officer Terraine on 19 June, and Taffy Williams four days later, squat and hearty and with a wide repertoire of rugger songs.

Tension dwindled slightly, and Perowne experienced relief and even thankfulness that France had suffered her fate. He now believed that Britain alone might stand a greater chance of survival, rather than when tied to a corpse. For the moment, it seemed that both the Luftwaffe and the RAF were catching breath for the next stage. He read the Air Ministry weekly Intelligence Summary dated 27 June which declared, 'Since the 21st, there has been a very sharp drop in German Air Force activity, and it is probable that units are being rested in order to consolidate and to retain a high proportion of serviceability.' The majority of German raids took place during darkness, and Perowne's squadron was not involved in attempted counter-operations. The Fighter Command Intelligence Report pointed out on 28 June that the present raids were probably intended as disruptive and nuisance-value strikes, and also to train enemy pilots in navigational techniques.

Perowne's pilots continued their Channel patrols and, at the same time, to prepare for the expected renewed offensive. Many hours were spent flying simulated dog-fights above the airfield, attempting to formulate the hard-earnd experience gained over France. Perowne introduced new tactics, worked out in conjunction with George whose methodical mind he found increasingly useful. Following the looser V formation which had already been put into practice, the Squadron-Leader now allotted different roles to the sections flying an attack or patrol sortie: one section, to be led by Lex or Simon, would be stationed, wherever possible, about 1,000 feet above and behind the other aircraft, flying a weaving course to keep watch for the enemy.

The lull affected each pilot in different ways, all observed by Perowne with his customary vigilance. George accepted the lessened activity as a matter of course, and he practised his flying with cool and rigorous determination, usually engaged in mock dogfights with Womack, equally unemotional; Lex became quieter, and Perowne hoped that his recklessness might have begun to ebb; by the end of June, Simon had become bored, disappearing off to Town to his latest girl, or lolling with his feet up in dispersal and complaining loudly that it was about time the whistle blew for the second half. Joe remained reserved, but in some way most useful of all to Perowne: his sheer love of flying, combined with his high degree of skill, made him an excellent teacher for the newcomers; Joe was always the first to volunteer for dogfight practice, and Perowne often watched the youngster as he looped and soared and spiralled above the beeches, with the Spitfire seeming like a bird in the midst of a courtship display.

At other times, Joe slipped away to the farm, which apparently he liked to visit. Perowne tried to guess what the farm had to offer – perhaps only the girl whose name he'd heard mentioned – and Perowne wondered if she were as gentle and expressive as the boy. Simon teased his friend, saying Joe didn't dare show her to anyone for fear of competition: Joe merely smiled good-naturedly. Perowne couldn't decide whether time spent at the farm would be beneficial or otherwise for the pilot: Joe seemed more relaxed and his eyes less anxious, yet the family atmosphere and the girl's influence might give the false impression that the lull would continue indefinitely.

Joe still tried to keep away from the farm. One night in the last week of June, he even went with Simon in his battered car to London, rather than go to the Barrett's. Simon told him, 'The binge will do you good – too much fresh air on that dratted farm will make you giddy. Come and meet Lucy.' They met Simon's girl in Trafalgar Square, where Lucy waited with another blonde, and the four of them walked arm-in-arm to eat at Rule's, where Simon scandalized army officers at the next table with his boisterous love-making. Lucy seemed accustomed to it all, reacting in giggling and responsive fashion, while Joe grinned self-consciously and wondered how to behave with his partner for the evening.

She seemed amused by his reticence. He drank too much, and could scarcely remember going with the others to Lucy's small flat, and Simon disappearing with Lucy into the bedroom; his awareness returned with the warmth of the other girl's skin and the tightness of her thighs as she wound her legs around his naked body, and her sighs as she reached her climax. She continued to grasp him, moving her hips until he followed her, and then she held him, almost protectively. 'You didn't want to do that did you?'

Joe hesitated, then shook his head as he lay against her breast.

'I guessed not,' she said. 'But I did.'

He remained silent, and after a moment she added, defensively, 'I don't do it all the time, you know – I'm not like that.'

'Then why did you do it?'

She laughed, fresh and honest. 'You're not a big-head, are you? Other men would've thought it was because they were so handsome. I did it because I wanted to, and because I think, deep down, you did too. It's a bit of comfort, isn't it?'

'I suppose so.' Joe felt warm and still sleepy; her skin glowed in the light from the table-lamp above them, and her thighs felt moist and unprotected around his own. He said, 'I can't even remember your name.'

She laughed again. 'I suppose that's a compliment, since I'll bet you'll remember the rest of me. I'm Christine – most people call me Chris.'

'Hello Chris.' His head still rested on her full breast, and he could feel the heart-beat close to his mouth. Her hand lay lightly on her other breast, and he lifted his own hand to trace his finger-tips over her knuckles and down the fingers to the smooth curve beyond; she slid her hand away, and his lips moved over her skin, tasting the faint saltiness. The girl's loins stirred beneath him, and he moved the short, waiting distance into her again.

Only when he'd finished did he really look at her face, almost unwillingly. Her eyes were wide and frank, blue, flecked with greens and greys; her lips were parted, creased at the corner through laughter. 'Feel better?'

He smiled. 'Thanks to you.'

'Good. So do I. Now I'll make a cuppa, if you'll let me go. You may be skinny, but you can still be a weight.'

Joe rolled to one side, and she stretched, arching her

back, then scrambled up and stood over him for a moment as he lay amidst their crumpled clothing on the floor. She smiled down at him, then turned and walked to the kitchen, and he watched the bounce of her blonde hair against her neck, the shortness of the cut emphasising her nakedness, and he remembered the sweep of Susie's long fair hair as it fell gently across her face and shoulders, to flow down her slender back.

Susie waited for him to visit them again, yet still wondered if she wanted him to return. The BBC spoke of decreased enemy activity, but her father merely grunted and said it wouldn't last much longer and they'd better expect the worst. Peter grumbled good-naturedly that Joe must be frightened of hard work after the day he had helped in the orchard. He said one day, 'I never realized before how easy it was with two. I miss him.'

The twins were working in the top orchard again, and Joe hadn't been for almost a week. Birds fluttered in the trees above Susie's head, sparrows darting from branch to branch, and above the orchard, the house-martins from the barn-eaves flicked backwards and forwards; Susie's father said it promised to be a long, dry summer.

Joe came again at the start of July, and Susie noticed immediately that his shyness had built up once more. He arrived during the late afternoon, this time on a noisy motor-bike which sent the hens scuttling from the yard, and which seemed ill-suited to his frail figure. He stayed for supper, and talked readily to Susie's father and to Peter, but Susie noticed that he still preferred to ask questions about the farm rather than answering Peter's persistent queries.

'How's Mops?' asked Susie.

'She's fine. Having a bit of a rest, like all of us – and getting spoiled to death.'

Susie's mother turned from the sink, drying her hands. 'You could do with more sun on you, boy. And more meat on your bones. Come here more often, and we'll fatten you up.'

Next day the latest Fighter Command Intelligence Report declared, 'There are indications that an enemy sea and airborne expedition is in an advanced stage of preparation.' And on 3 July, Perowne received additional information. 'Enemy reconnaissance has shown a marked increase. There is evidence that surface craft suitable for assisting landing parties have been prepared.' Twenty-four hours later, Stukas attacked Atlantic Convoy OA 178 off Portland, sinking four vessels and damaging nine, and during the next days, these strikes against Channel shipping steadily increased, combined with further evidence of possible imminent invasion.

Perowne's squadron remained uninvolved, with the main enemy operations in the Channel being launched in 12 Group Fighter Command area, further west along the south coast. But Perowne believed that one or two days would probably see an end to the lull, and within a week the invasion might have begun. He felt no sense of apprehension, but rather an impatience for the wait to finish; yet the parallel fear for Anna grew stronger, and he drove up to London on 9 July for only the third visit which he'd allowed himself since the fall of France.

His decision to go was made only at the last moment; he tried to telephone his wife, but with no success, and he arrived to find the flat empty. He walked slowly through the five rooms, savouring the peace of the place and the sense of shared possession with Anna, and above all her unseen presence – the underwear scattered on the unmade bed, the breakfast plates piled in the sink, the book laying open and face down on the arm of the sofa.

He climbed the stairs to the studio in the attic, and sat for a moment in Anna's chair. Light slanted onto an unfinished canvas, catching the vermilion in the flowers. The room seemed so quiet, totally unlike any to which he'd become accustomed; even the privacy of his own quarters at the squadron was never free from echoing voices and feet in the corridors.

The door clicked in the hall of the flat. Perowne waited in silence. Anna suddenly called his name, and he made no reply but began to walk down the stairs. She ran up to him, throwing her arms around his waist and hugging tight, her delighted laughter half-smothered against him.

'How did you know I was here?' he asked.

'I didn't. I just sensed it as soon as I walked in. Why didn't you tell me you were coming?' She led him into the living room, still chattering. 'I had to go to a nursing talk, and I haven't had a chance to tidy this mess.'

She sat on the floor against him, her head on his knee, long legs bent under her, and he asked, 'What was the talk about?'

'Oh, I'm getting very advanced. They say I'm proficient now.'

'For what?'

She laughed. 'Not that – or at least, I am – I hope.' She suddenly bent her arm behind his knee and gripped him hard, pressing her cheek againt his thigh. 'Oh, why don't you come more often?'

'Because I'd never want to leave.'

'I want you so much. And it's so damned lonely in that huge bed.'

'We'll fill it in a moment. First tell me what else you're proficient at.'

'The nursing thing – the section leader says I'm ready.

For the bombing, I suppose he means. It all seems so horrible, and yet not as ghastly as it might, because it doesn't seem real. Only a year ago, we were on holiday, and everything seemed so grand. It can't have changed that much.' She reached to the table. 'And look at this daft thing they've just issued.'

Perowne took the Ministry of Information leaflet. He read the title: 'What to do if the Parachutists should come,' and further down: 'The order is to stay put . . . Do not believe rumours and do not spread them . . . Be calm, quick, exact. Keep watch . . . When parachutists come down near homes, they will not be feeling very brave . . .'

Anna interrupted his reading. 'I think I'll stick it on the wall. It'll cheer me up when I'm gloomy and missing you.' She stood, and took hold of both his hads to pull him up. 'Now, come on. I can't wait any longer.' He followed her through into the bedroom for the love-making, which she seemed to demand even more than he, and he didn't know whether to be frightened or proud by the extent of her need for him.

At 4.15 next morning, Perowne received the order for his sections to scramble in support of No 74 Squadron Spitfires engaging the enemy over the Channel. The six aircraft rose through the low clouds to the early sunlight beyond, heading south, only to be returned to the airfield after forty minutes: the dogfights between 74 Squadron aircraft and Dornier bombers had ended. Throughout the morning Perowne received reports of other actions, mainly off Yarmouth, and according to Group Control, 'It seems as if things are starting to happen.'

Soon after 1 pm, he led two sections up again, this time to provide cover for a convoy already being escorted by Hurricanes from No 32 Squadron, Biggin Hill. Extra protection had been ordered, following reports from several radar stations that enemy aircraft were assembling over the Calais area.

Simon led the second section, with Joe flying as his Number Two. Visibility was now clear. The aircraft climbed for height immediately above the airfield, and by the time Perowne reached Ashford, the Spitfires had risen to around 12,000 feet. The Controller's voice suddenly sounded loud over the R/T from Biggin Hill sector station. 'Hello, Piper Leader. Estimated 25 bandits 15 miles east of Calais. 10,000 feet climbing, going north.'

Perowne replied, 'OK, Zona. Message received.' And to the squadron pilots, he ordered, 'Climb Angels 15. Come on, let's welcome the blighters.' The two sections immediately increased their angle of ascent.

Joe listened to the steady throb of his engine, attempting to gain comfort from the familiar sound, yet his stomach still heaved. At least two dozen enemy aircraft were approaching, against only six of them. The Spitfires crossed the coast east of Dungeness, and soon afterwards, Joe could see a staggered line of vessels 16,000 feet below – the convoy making its way eastwards up the Channel.

Almost immediately, rings of white water suddenly appeared between the ships, and tiny black specks were darting and wheeling around the convoy formation. Perowne called, 'They're already attacking. Let's have a look round before we join in.' The Spitfires maintained formation for a moment longer, with the pilots tipping their aircraft wings attempting to discover enemy fighters protecting the dive-bombers below.

'OK, Piper aircraft. Here we go.'

One by one, the Spitfires in front of Joe flicked to

starboard and into their dives – Perowne, George, Taffy, then a slight gap before Simon broke away, then Joe followed with Johnny at the rear. Down they went, with the air speed shooting up, and details of the fighting emerging clearer. Joe identified the German aircraft as Stukas, and he tried to seek reassurance from words which George had said – the dive bombers were easy targets for Spitfires once the enemy had broken formation. Immediately to the front of Simon's aircraft, three of them were pulling out of a dive, ragged and struggling to regain height.

'Tally ho!' shouted Simon, and Joe noticed tracer erupt from his aircraft wings. Simon dived straight towards the centre of the Stuka trio; Joe banked slightly to port, aiming for the last in the line, and he acted almost unthinkingly, carried along by the movement and unable to deviate, trusting entirely in his Spitfire. The enemy aircraft seemed to fly directly through his flaying tracer bullets. He eased back the stick, and his Spitfire surged upwards. He looked frantically for Simon, knowing it was his task to stay with the section leader; to one side he spotted an aircraft twisting slowly down belching smoke – a Stuka – and someone was screaming, 'He's mine! Jesus, he's mine!' Joe thought the voice sounded like Taffy, flying his first operational flight. Ahead, he could see another Stuka still trying to gain altitude, and he pulled in behind, glancing in the mirror to check the rear, but seeing nothing. He closed to about 200 yards and pressed the button for a two-second burst. His bullets missed the Stuka, and he altered deflection and fired another burst, longer this time, and the bullets clipped the German's tail. Chunks flew away on either side, and the Stuka immediately twisted away to port. Joe was about to pursue when Simon's voice shouted in his ears. 'Orange Two! Break! Break! Hun behind!'

At the same instant, tracer danced past Joe's cockpit; he threw the Spitfire to starboard; the Me 109 on his tail flashed by, just a few feet above. He continued in a tight turn, and another 109 dived down in front of him, and all at once the sky seemed thick with them. Joe recognized Simon's voice again over the jumble of shouts on the R/T. 'Climb, Orange Section. Climb like hell.' A Spitfire was diving to Joe's right, flames gushing from the base of its wings.

Then a Messerschmitt pulled from its dive in front of Joe and levelled towards him. The two aircraft were heading directly towards each other, and Joe knew that the first to pull away would be shot to splinters by the other. His fingers were slippery with sweat as they clung to the stick, and he hunched himself down in his seat, whispering to his Spitfire, 'Come on. Take me. Don't let me go.' Vivid flashes flamed from the Messerschmitt's guns, but the range remained too far and the bullets fell low. Then Joe fired. The effect was terrible. The German aircraft disintegrated as Joe's .303 bullets tore into the engine and cockpit, then the Spitfire flew almost directly into the burning wreckage and debris clattered on its cockpit cover. When Joe flashed through to the open sky, the streams of oil from the German fighter were streaked over his perspex like black blood.

He took his Spitfire in a steady climbing turn into the empty sky, whispering again, 'We're alive.' He looked down and could see the shapeless flaming mass falling slowly towards the sea. He turned to fly back to the airfield, and wondered how old the German pilot had been, if he had been as frightened, if he'd shared the same stupid thoughts. Joe remembered that when he'd buckled on his boots that morning, he'd wondered if he should ever undo them again, and if he should ever clean his teeth again, and whether it was worth cleaning them anyway. When he closed the door to his room, he'd feared that it might be for the last time, and he'd turned and walked back to open it again, just to prove himself wrong. Joe wished he knew whether the German had really wanted to fire or just to break away unhurt, like he himself.

His Spitfire came in gently to land and he could see Simon waiting for him on the grass, holding Mops by the collar. Perowne had already come back; the rest followed one by one, except for Johnny. Three German aircraft had been shot down for certain – by George, Taffy and Joe – with another two probables; Lex led a second sortie during the late afternoon, but came back without another victim to his credit. Reports of other engagements in the Channel area continued throughout the afternoon, and it seemed clear that the Luftwaffe had launched an intensified offensive against Channel shipping – perhaps a prelude to invasion. Perowne knew that time for preparations had ended, and that the squadron must fight as it now stood. The lull had brought improvements, but he also knew that these could never be sufficient.

'I killed today,' said Joe. Susie glanced up quickly from her baking bowl. 'He was my first – at least, the first I can be certain about.' Susie didn't know what to say; the two of them were alone in the farmhouse kitchen, and Susie felt relieved that Peter was still seeing to the cows, since she would have hated to hear his delight at Joe's news. She noticed the way Joe held one hand against the other when he raised his match to his cigarette, and then carefully placed the spent stick in a neat line next to the others in the ashtray. They sat in silence, except for brief snatches of conversation, and Joe went after only twenty five minutes, saying he had to be back at the airfield. Susie sensed that he was unsure of himself alone with her.

Later, the family sat together in the kitchen, and as usual Susie's father switched on the wireless to hear the news. The announcer reported the words of Sir Edward Grigg, Parliamentary Secretary at the Ministry of Information, spoken earlier in the Commons. 'This afternoon, one of the greatest air battles of the war took place; tonight, many bombers may be over our towns. Tonight, thousands of our soldiers will be on the alert, waiting for an attack which may come in several places at dawn.' Then the family listened to a recording made by BBC reporter Charles Gardner at Dover during the day, describing the dogfights which had then been taking place just out from the Channel. Susie could hear the faint stuttering of the guns. 'There's one coming down in flames – there's somebody hit a German – and he's coming down – there's a long streak . . . Oh boy, I've never seen anything so good as this – the RAF fighters have really got these boys taped!'

Susie walked out of the room, Nellie padding at her heels, and she stood in the quiet of the yard feeling the night breeze on her cheeks. Threats of invasion still seemed so unreal. The recording of dogfights above Dover seemed theatrical, until she remembered the quivering flame as Joe lifted his match to the cigarette.

CHAPTER NINE

Joe woke with his head still throbbing, and with the orderly shaking his shoulder, repeating, 'Come on, sir, come on – it's gone 3.15.' The yellow light from the bulb directly above the bed seared into his eyes as he tried to keep them open. He shivered as he sat up and reached for his clothes. Simon had fallen asleep again, with the blankets rumpled up over his head. Joe struggled from the sheets, flinching as his feet found the cold floor, and he dressed as quickly as he could – Irvin trousers over his pyjamas, sweater, flying boots, scarf, Irvin jacket. He prodded Simon, and merely received a grunt in reply, then he hunched on his Mae West, and pulling back the corner of the blackout, wiped the condensation from the window, and peered outside. Dawn had begun to split the night sky into areas of pale green.

Simon stirred behind him. 'Another bloody fine day,' he muttered in disgust. 'We'll be busy again.'

Joe could see the Spitfires waiting further down the field near dispersal, and he heard an airscrew being turned slowly by a starter battery. Suddenly, the engine woke into a shattering roar which sent the rooks wheeling from the beeches.

He left Simon still dressing, and walked down the corridor, out into the morning air. He felt snug in his Irvin suit, and his boots glistened with the heavy dew as he crossed the grass to his Spitfire. The fitter was climbing from the wing, and Joe called 'good morning' over the sound of the engine, then climbed up to check the cockpit, cold seeping through his thick clothing from the blast of the propeller. He examined the instruments one by one, comforted by the familiar routine and by the renewed contact with his aircraft, then he eased himself out of the cockpit, noted that his parachute was waiting for him on the wing, jumped to the ground, and walked to dispersal.

An orderly knelt by the stove trying to light the stubborn fire. Lex, Taffy and George were already in the hut; Simon wandered in, slumped into a deckchair, and immediately fell asleep again; Tommy Terraine entered to complete the two-section strength, and the wait began – the mixture of boredom and tension which seemed to ebb and flow in waves, each time with fear stronger as the inevitable moment approached. The clock on the wooden wall seemed to stand still, then jerk forward from one quarter hour to another.

Lex sat at the table with the newspaper spread in front of him and a pencil in his hand, wondering how long he could maintain the pretence of trying to complete the crossword. The grubby border to the newsprint was already covered with doodles; his coffee mug stood empty by his elbow, and he wanted another drink to ease his constricted throat, yet he hesitated to ask the orderly, since it might be suggested that his thirst came from fear.

Sorties to protect convoys had been flown on an average of three times a day for the last one and a half weeks. Only the previous 48 hours had brought some respite when widespread fog had been followed by a thick overcast, to reduce air activity. Today, the forecast threatened brighter weather, with showers – sufficient cloud to give the enemy cover, sufficient clear sky to allow the enemy to attack the shipping.

Lex had failed to kill since the fall of France, and his lack of success stoked his fear. Each sortie, he sought to destroy with even greater desperation in the effort to push aside his own destruction. Now, after the enforced inactivity of the past two days which had prevented his terror from finding release, he felt more naked and vulnerable than ever. Others had obtained victims – Perowne, Womack, George, Tommy Terraine, Simon. If they could, why not he? And during the same period, Henny had been wounded again, and Dent had gone. Lex knew he must soon follow. He had no expectation of surviving the next few hours, yet continued to hope, and this hope caused his terror.

The order to scramble came at 8.30, after a wait of nearly five hours in the dingy dispersal hut. Lex felt numbed apprehension as he sprinted for his aircraft, grabbed his parachute, and flung himself into the hated cockpit. They found the enemy 5,000 feet above the Channel south of Folkestone, twenty or more 109s with the morning sun behind them, and the Spitfires immediately climbed to attack, with Lex leading the first section, and Joe his Number Two. Lex gave himself no time to think. Instead, he rivetted his attention on one enemy aircraft, boosted his engine and jerked his stick still harder into his stomach, at the same time shouting over the R/T, 'Let the bastards have it!'

Within ten seconds, the sky seemed crammed with weaving aircraft and streaking tracer fire. Lex continued to fling his machine one way then the other to keep the enemy in his sights, firing repeated bursts, and cursing the German for continuing to fly. The 109 in front of him dived, and Lex plummeted after, the sea filling his vision as he dropped almost vertically. The 109 seemed to be gaining ground; Lex stabbed the button in a frantic gesture of despair, to find his ammunition gone, and the 109 levelled unscathed to skim away above the waves. Lex uttered a sound which seemed both a sob and an oath as he banked to port towards the coast.

A sudden jolt shook his cockpit and jarred his back hard against the seat, and a huge black fist seemed to close over the perspex then lift again as the 109 swept above him. Lex twisted the Spitfire into a half-roll to pull away from his attacker, and the movement caused the wetness to flood faster down his face: he believed for an instant that the moisture must be blood, until the stinging sweat trickled into his eyes. He climbed and glanced half over his shoulder to see the 109 climbing with him, and he jerked his head to the front again to see another aircraft diving in a sweeping curve towards him. He sobbed with relief when he noted the smooth lines of a Spitfire, and at the same moment, Joe's quiet voice came over the R/T.

'Dive, Orange One. Dive.'

Lex pushed forward the column, and the Spitfire flashed above him with tracer already bursting from the wings. Ahead he could see the coastline with the houses of Folkestone seeming to beckon him to safety as his aircraft raced over the swell towards the beach.

Joe forgot his fear as his Spitfire followed the 109, and his thumb sent the bursts of fire after the twisting enemy. Smoke began to flutter from the German aircraft and the nose of the machine tilted forward, lifted, then dropped again into a deeper dive. Joe narrowed the gap; he fired one more burst, then lifted his thumb. The enemy aircraft continued to struggle for height, and Joe knew he should administer the kill. Yet he felt unable; the enemy seemed already useless, and to fire further would simply be murder. Smoke issued thicker from the Messerschmitt. Joe saw the cockpit cover slide back, and the pilot slowly moving into the opening. Suddenly, the German jerked backwards as the wind caught him, the tiny figure somersaulting over the smoking tail of the 109 and into the clear air, then the Messerschmitt flipped forward in its death dive to the sea, Joe circled, returning to the widening patch of white where the aircraft had disappeared, and now a parachute floated down, drifting north in the direction of the shore. Joe banked closer, and he could see the pilot's face turned towards him; he wondered if the other man was experiencing relief at his deliverance from the aircraft, fear as he swayed towards the sea, or thankfulness that captivity might soon end his war. Already, Joe's fear had started to return.

Patrols and sudden engagements over the Channel convoys continued into the third week of July, with the level of activity dependent on the weather. Most days dawned fine, although haze persisted over the Channel. Tension remained strong; Lex had still to obtain another kill, and Simon had even begun to tease the New Zealander about his 'spell of bad luck'. Simon himself gained two more victims, on 21 and 24 July. On the latter date, George returned from the afternoon sortie with two kills and one probable. Meanwhile, the faces in the mess underwent further change. Sergeant Andy Maclean came one evening and died next morning, and many pilots in the squadron hadn't heard him speak a sentence; Terraine died over Hythe; Womack lay in Ashford hospital, his legs heavily bandaged after his parachute dragged him across the roof of a greenhouse near Rye; Pilot Officer Treleaven had recently arrived, his Devon burr revealing his native county almost as much as his name.

Perowne shuffled the names constantly on his lists, trying to spare strength yet still undertake the patrols requested of him; and anxious lest the squadron should suffer too much before the next stage. He knew the next phase must soon begin; attacks on Channel convoys, arduous though they were for his pilots, must surely be intended as a preliminary. Intelligence reports still spoke of invasion; the main Luftwaffe units were believed to be organizing for all-out war. On 28 July, he read the latest Fighter Command Survey which declared, 'It is considered that the RAF, while still not brought up to full serviceability, is once more strong enough to begin a large-scale offensive, although it is doubtful whether advanced aerodromes have yet been supplied with sufficient stores of bombs, fuel and ammunition to carry out sustained operations.' Meanwhile the pilots continued to study the dawn each morning, attempting to discover whether cloud might prolong survival.

On 29 July, night clouds slipped away to reveal a fine morning, with Met reporting clear visibility apart from haze clinging to the Channel. Simon led the first sortie, returning with no contact having been made. Early in the afternoon, Perowne and a second section led by Lex were scrambled after Control declared that about 60 enemy aircraft were moving across the Channel in the direction of Dover. Once more, Joe flew as Number Two to Lex; ten miles from the coast, the newcomer Treleaven banked away after having reported engine trouble and receiving instructions from Perowne to return home.

Almost immediately, Perowne observed the attack already taking place on Dover, with dive-bombers streaking down over the harbour, and smoke rising lazily from the quay area. He gave the order to engage, slipped forward his safety catch, and peeled to starboard, with the other two aircraft in his section following close behind; he shuffled himself firmer in his seat, and caught a Stuka in his quivering sights. At that moment, Lex sounded over the R/T. 'Hello, Piper

Leader. Huns high out to sea. Two dozen or more. Am going out.'

Perowne had no time to answer. His fire streaked below the Stuka as the enemy machine began to climb from the harbour, and he saw boats bobbing like corks amidst the bomb circles. He pulled back the stick to follow the enemy and at the same time, tried to contact Lex. 'Orange Leader – don't go out to sea' – but he heard no reply, and a moment later he had to throw his own aircraft into a dive; whilst he did so, he imagined Lex climbing to face the Huns above, vastly outnumbered, and he cursed his section leader for being a reckless fool. Lex would only have Joe to help him; they should all have stuck together. Even in the midst of his own twirling, sweating dogfight, Perowne continued to catch snatches over the R/T from the New Zealander and his Number Two.

'Stay with me, Joe.'

'I'm right behind.'

'Tallyho! ... I think I got him! Christ, here's another ... Stick with me, Joe ...'

Lex returned alone five minutes after Perowne had landed. His aircraft stopped, and he stood in the open cockpit waving his clasped hands above his head in a gesture of triumph. Perowne walked across the grass towards him.

'I got two! I'm back on the ball!'

'Where's Joe?'

'Oh, he's OK. His machine seemed a bit dicky after we'd crossed the coast, but he said he'd make it OK.'

Perowne felt his anger tightening the tired muscles on his face. 'What the hell did you leave him for?'

'I tell you he's fine – and you know what a bloody good pilot he is.'

'You should've come back with him, and you know that damn well.'

'Hell, he wanted to nurse his machine. He looks after that aeroplane as if it were a favourite horse – listen, what did I tell you? Here he comes.'

Perowne could hear the Spitfire approaching from the east; he snapped an order for Lex to wait in the squadron office, then stood on the grass, watching Joe turn in to land: the New Zealander shrugged, and walked back to dispersal. Perowne waited as Joe's aircraft taxied slowly to a halt and he noted the weariness on the youngster's face, and his effort to smile as he approached. Around the cockpit hung the smell of over-heated insulation. 'She'll be OK, I think,' said Joe, 'but I'll just wait for the fitter.'

Perowne shut the office door behind him; Lex leant against the littered desk. 'You're a damned fool, Lex. I've told you that before.'

'Why, for Christ's sake? He's back now.'

'Not only that. You chased out to sea with only Joe to help you, and against God only knows how many enemy.'

'I had to stop them coming at our arses.'

'You had to do nothing of the kind. You just wanted better pickings. Five of us – that's all there were. Five. God knows, that was few enough – without you flitting off for a private party, and risking not only your own damned neck but Joe's as well. You know he'd stick with you whatever bloody foolishness you led him into.'

Perowne's anger suddenly evaporated to be replaced with a resurgence of weariness. He sat behind the desk and took out his pipe. 'We'll forget it. We're all bloody tired.' He looked up at Lex, and made an effort to smile. 'But for pity's sake, try and remember that not all of us want to be heroes. Some of us aren't like you, Lex. We just want to survive as long as possible, and do our jobs, and not to imitate your cowboy stunts.'

Lex grinned back at him. 'I thought we needed to bring down the bastards.'

'And so we do. We, Lex – not just you. Remember one thing. As far as I'm concerned, the only figures that count are the squadron ones – the total of all successes by the boys together. I'm only interested in the squadron, Lex. I don't want any aces. Just a damned good squadron.'

Mist and drizzle swept across Kent and much of the south coast next day. Simon took up a section in the morning which shot down a German reconnaissance aircraft, with none of the three pilots being able to claim individual credit, since all of them had torn the Dornier like terriers at a rat.

Joe had been placed 'off state' whilst the mechanics checked over his aircraft. He borrowed Simon's car and drove to the farm, arriving before lunch and joining the family as they sat round the huge scrubbed table. He answered Peter's questions in his normal reluctant fashion; Susie noticed that he only seemed to become more responsive when he spoke of Simon.

'He's such a grand chap – as tough as they come. He won his Cambridge Blue for boxing, and he's got huge boxer's hands, yet he can fly his kite as gently as a dove. He'll stick up for anyone and hates gossip. He's a good friend.' Joe looked across the table at Susie, smiling as he continued, 'He's a funny bloke – very superstitious. He's got a dirty pink scarf with white spots, which he always insists on wearing when he flies – he's had it ever since he first climbed into a cockpit. One day, Lex hid it for a joke, and Simon wouldn't go near his aircraft till it appeared again. And another thing. Each night, he searches our room. Yes that's right; he actually gets down on his hands and knees and looks under the beds and in the lockers, regular as clockwork. When you ask him what on earth he's doing he just grins and says "There could be some Charleys lurking down there." I've never been able to find out what a Charley actually is. Lex teases him, but I don't bother.'

'What's Lex like?' asked Peter.

'Oh, he's OK. A New Zealander. His father has bags of money.' Joe began to eat again after his pause to describe Simon – the longest talk that Susie had ever heard from him. 'Lex is about the bravest in the squadron, next to Simon. He fools around a lot in the mess.' He hesitated, then added, 'The CO tore him off a strip yesterday for shooting off against too many Germans. He seems to want to take on the whole Luftwaffe himself. The CO's a good chap – very kind, a bit like a decent schoolmaster. He's got a beautiful wife. I've met her once or twice.'

Susie asked, 'How old is she?'

'About twenty-five, I suppose. They can't have been married very long. She's an artist, though she looks more like a model. Very dark and creamy. All the pilots rave about her – especially Simon, although goodness knows he's got enough girls of his own.' Joe looked down at his plate again, and returned to being cheerfully noncommital.

The month ended quietly with the lull continuing into August during unsettled, unpredictable weather. Even the fine periods brought reduced Luftwaffe activity, renewing speculation over German intentions. One evening, most of the pilots were drinking in the mess with the wireless switched on, and the BBC declared, 'Recent drops in enemy operations are said to be caused by the cloudy conditions over the German air bases in Occupied France. An Air Ministry spokesman commented today that the lull has enabled RAF Fighter Command to prepare itself for any eventuality, and the RAF has complete confidence in its ability to overcome any new tactic. The spokesman added that pilots were eager for battle to be resumed.'

'For Christ's sake turn that rubbish off,' shouted Taffy. Someone else called out, 'Sod the Air Ministry – nobody asked if I were bloody eager.' Perowne, standing with Simon at the bar, had already noticed how the waiting was beginning to affect the nerves of his pilots. No enemy aircraft had been seen by them for four days, although squadrons in the Portsmouth area had made some contact. Now Simon said, 'I wish the damn weather would clear, or the Germans would finish their mucking about or whatever they're up to. I'm fed up with sitting on my backside in that ruddy dispersal hut. And tomorrow's meant to be a Bank Holiday. Some holiday!'

'It may bring some excitement for you.'

Simon lifted his glass. 'Here's hoping. It's like waiting for the bell to ring.'

'Which round?'

Simon grinned as he pushed across his empty glass. 'I was waiting for that – yours if you say so. I'll have the same again.'

Joe, Simon, Taffy and Chris Treleaven waited for three hours in the dispersal hut next morning before being scrambled to locate a reconnaissance aircraft; they searched until lack of fuel brought them back to the airfield, where they sat outside in the sunshine while their aircraft were refuelled, and the waiting continued. Simon read out a statement by Churchill which had appeared in the newspaper that Saturday morning. 'The fact that the Germans are now putting about rumours that they do not intend an invasion should be regarded with a double dose of the suspicion which attaches to all their utterances. Our sense of growing strength and preparedness must not lead to the slightest relaxation of vigilance.'

Taffy lolled in his deckchair, punctuating Simon's reading with massive simulated snores; Chris played darts against an improvised board chalked on the dispersal hut wall, and the repeated thud of the points into wood steadily aggravated Joe's frayed nerves. He turned his face into the slight breeze, trying to cool himself, and he could hear Mops panting by his feet.

The weather remained sunny over the Bank Holiday, but began to break at the start of the following week, and by Monday evening, the clouds had opened. Susie stood in the porch watching the rain turning the dust in the yard to grey mud running in rivulets through the cobbles. The BBC nine o'clock news declared that, even with the cloudy conditions, four enemy aircraft had been shot down during the day, with another four unconfirmed; one British pilot was reported missing.

Joe arrived at the farm late the following afternoon. This time he sat in the passenger seat of the ancient open car, and another man sat behind the wheel. Peter rattled down the bucket he was carrying, and ran across the yard to open the gate; Susie called Nellie to her as the car drove noisily in. The stranger climbed out of the seat without bothering to open the door: he was tall and bulky, too big it seemed for the car; a flop of fair hair fell down almost to one eye, and he kept pushing it back impatiently; he had an angular face, both attractive and ugly, with a nose that seemed to Susie as if it had once been broken, and his smile revealed uneven teeth. He clapped Peter on the shoulder, and strode across to Susie, hand outstretched, a wide grin across his lively face.

'This is Simon,' said Joe.

'I guessed it was.'

Simon squeezed her hand tight. 'So this is where Joe hides himself? I'm not surprised.'

'He's told us about you.'

'Has he, by God. The mean devil. I'd rather have that pleasure myself.'

'We've come to invite you for a ride,' said Joe. 'Just for an hour or so, then we have to be back.'

They drove down the Maidstone road, then turned into the narrow country lanes up into the North Downs, winding between the beech woods, with the Vale of Kent spreading green behind them. Splashes of sunlight moved swiftly over the slopes and glinted on the broad curves of the Medway. The twins sat in the back of the car, with Peter bending forward to chatter to the pilots in the front while Susie leant against the leather seat to feel the wind on her face.

'I need a drink,' called Simon over his shoulder, and they stopped at a pub on the top of the Downs. They sat in the garden in the patterned shade of the trees, and Simon brought out the glasses on a tray; Susie sipped her cider and listened to the quick succession of questions put to Simon by her brother, and to his amiable answers. Then Joe stood and walked away from the table with his beer mug in his hand, and after a moment, Susie followed him. Joe was sitting on the edge of the lawn, where the ground began to slope thick with bracken down to the valley. Susie sat beside him. 'You should have brought Mops,' she said.

'I nearly did. She doesn't see enough of me.'

To their right, the view stretched round the curve of the Downs towards Sevenoaks and the distant blue woods of Westerham; they could smell the tang of a charcoal-burner's fire, and the wetness of the ferns beneath the trees.

'He's a good pilot you know,' said Joe suddenly. 'He's shot down goodness knows how many.' Susie was watching a ladybird creeping up her ankle: it had crawled over her bare foot, and it half-opened its bright wings as if to fly, before changing its mind and moving forward again.

'Don't you ever wear shoes?' he asked her.

She smiled. 'Not often. I don't like them.' After a pause, she added, 'Simon doesn't seem a bit like you.'

'No. Perhaps that's why we're such good friends. He came to the squadron just before me, and looked after me from the start. He's one of the kindest fellows I've ever met – wouldn't hurt a soul, and always a good word for everyone.'

The ladybird still moved busily on Susie's leg below her knee. Joe suddenly reached forward, and gently put his fingers before it, and his hand felt cool on Susie's skin; after a moment's hesitation, the insect climbed onto his fingers, but almost immediately, it opened the tiny wings and was gone. 'Simon doesn't seem to feel any fear,' he said.

'Perhaps he does underneath.'

'I don't think so. He says it's like boxing or rugger. You just have to get stuck in without thinking about it. I can't seem to do it. But he has no nerves, and doesn't give a damn.'

'If he isn't frightened, he can't be brave. If he has no fear, he hasn't got anything to struggle with inside him.'

Joe looked at her. She was still gazing down into the valley, her hair half-hiding her eyes. He reached over, and she felt his fingers gently smooth back a long strand then rest for a moment on her cheek. 'Come on,' he said 'We'd better rescue Simon from all the questions.' She took his hand and he helped her up.

Day by day, Susie found the news bulletins increasingly unbearable. Two pilots missing – one, three, and on one day, five. She tried not to listen, but her fear remained. She told herself that Joe was still a stranger, yet it made no difference; she felt ashamed of the anger she felt towards him for unconsciously feeding her concern. Sometimes, she hoped he'd return and ease for a while her fears for him; at others, she wished he'd never come again.

And so, when Susie saw the car emerge from the woods down the lane one afternoon, she put down her broom and almost ran from the yard and into the fields. She slowed while Nellie caught her up, panting, then walked on away from the farm and the young pilot. She wandered down through the orchard, round the meadow and into the beech wood, passing the rotten swing which the twins used when they were children, and walking on towards the stream, all the while knowing that her attempted escape was ridiculous and childish. She sat for a moment on the bank of the stream, looking into the fast-running water, with her knees bent up under her chin. She remembered the days she had spent with Peter, trying to catch minnows and sticklebacks in jam-jar traps, and how they'd carried the silvery fish in triumph back to the farm, and how disappointed she'd been when the fish soon died. Those days didn't seem too far away, yet the gap between then and now was a chasm.

Joe might die at any moment. That fact was inescapable. He might go as suddenly as he had arrived, and anyone who knew him must be prepared for his departure, even though no preparation could remove the fear. She walked back through the wood, beginning to hurry, afraid he might have left before she reached the farmhouse; then, as she made her way through the orchard, she saw Mops in front of her, nose down and trying to follow the scent that she and Nellie had left. Susie called and Mops bounced up, barking and with tail weaving, and they entered the yard together.

Joe drove back to the airfield an hour later, returning along lanes where the dust hung chalky-white in the sunsplashes beneath the trees, and he made a fresh resolve never to visit the farm again. Something which Peter had just said made him believe he would be selfish to go. The boy had mentioned the daily casualty figures on the BBC, and how they all listened even more closely than before, joking about wanting to know each day how many Joe had shot down. Perhaps Peter had meant what he said, but Joe realized now that Susie listened with increasing anxiety. And she'd tried to avoid him. Joe knew fear could be contagious. He carried it with him to infect all those who had the misfortune to meet him; he felt dirty with his disease, and even more lonely. Only his Spitfire really provided comfort, and yet the aircraft would be the instrument to carry him to death.

CHAPTER TEN

Lex repeatedly stared at the convoy 7,000 feet below, and cursed the vessels for moving so slowly. The six ships seemed stationary until Lex checked with the coastline and noticed that Hastings had now become a smudge on the horizon. He banked his Spitfire again to lead his section in another circle around the plodding vessels, and he said to himself, 'Why don't the bastards pull their fingers out? We just sit up here like a flaming Aunt Sally.' He checked his fuel again, and noted with disappointment that another ten minutes patrolling time remained. Lex almost wanted the Germans to come to put an end to the waiting.

Taffy flew three wings' span to the right of Lex. His eyes were sore from searching in the sun for enemy air-craft, and he felt increasing disappointment that no Germans had appeared. He wanted another victim, to bring his total to five, and his confidence remained strong: each of his kills had been obtained so easily, and as he'd told Womack, 'Man, they're so stupid. Especially those lovely Stukas. Once they've dropped their goodies, it's like popping off crows as they flap up from the nest.' Taffy had never realized it would be so easy; he grinned to himself as he thought of the complicated diagrams which Womack and George delighted in dood-ling as they attempted to improve their tactics. 'You don't need tactics boyo – you just need to get stuck in and teach those Huns how to fly.'

Henny Fowler made up the section trio, his slight figure seeming too small for the cockpit seat. He con-stantly jerked his head in all directions, and he suffered the extra unease which always accompanied the normal apprehension when he flew with Lex. He didn't trust the New Zealander. 'Trying to be a bloody hero. At our expense. I'm not going to get myself brought down so that he can be a bloody ace. Not on your nellie.' His arm still ached from the wound he'd received on 7 June, and he realized to his surprise that exactly two months had gone since the first flight. He checked his instruments again, then spoke to Lex. 'Hello, Orange Leader. My fuel's getting low.'

'OK, Orange Two. We're all the same. Better wait till the next party arrives.' Two minutes later, six Hurricanes from No. 111 Squadron floated up to join them, and Lex led his Spitfires home. Ten minutes after landing, the pilots were informed that fierce dogfights were taking place over the convoy, involving ten British and fifteen Luftwaffe aircraft; two Hurricanes were shot down and two Me110s.

George explained his theory to Perowne at the mess bar, and to his own analytical mind, it all seemed so simple. 'They just want to tempt us out over the Channel, and then pick us off. Weaken us. Try to tire us out. Meanwhile, keep us waiting.'

'For what?'

'Invasion. They need control of the air for the troops to obtain a beach-head, and this way, they could get it. We're just wasting our strength – first, with helping the French; now, with protecting the convoys. There's a steady drain on both pilots and aircraft – just what the Germans want. We're conforming exactly to their plan. We should ignore the convoys, and stay on the ground, preserving our strength.'

'But we can't just let the ships get sunk.'

George shrugged. 'Which is more important – a few

111

coastal ships carrying coal, timber, goodness knows what, or Fighter Command – the best defence against invasion? It's simply a question of priorities. And the powers above have got the priorities wrong.'

Next day, the first air raid was experienced at Maidstone. Joe's fear for Susie, with the farm only six miles from the town, persuaded him to break his resolve and he promised himself a visit to the farm next evening, after his day's 'stand to'. Perowne shared similar apprehension for Anna, and he read again the Air Ministry weekly situation report issued this Thursday, 8 August. 'Prisoners of war say that the German people almost pity us, because we do not realize to the full, the terrific might of the attack when it does come. They think that the aeroplanes will come over in waves of at least 1,000 at a time, and that they will pulverize all objectives.' He wished again that Anna would leave London, but she still refused to recognize the need, and insisted on continuing to practise her nursing. 'All the better to look after you in your old age, my love,' she'd said.

The lull continued. One, two, three then four days, with tension steadily rising, and with the atmosphere of waiting becoming almost stifling. Perowne sensed the uneasiness in the mess; singing sessions no longer took place, and instead, George played the piano with the room almost silent. All the pilots seemed to feel that something was about to happen, yet it was impossible to guess what this something would be; and meanwhile, the small but steady numbers of Fighter Command pilots shot down over the Channel each day seemed to confirm George's theory; Perowne could only be thankful that none of these losses was suffered by his own squadron. He tried to allow his pilots as much rest as possible, but the patrols had to be continued. He himself snatched another evening in London with Anna; Simon, Lex and Taffy went up to Town on two successive nights; Joe went to the farm again, but only briefly, and Perowne wondered if the youngster had begun at last to tire of his visits. And all the while, Perowne tried to calculate when, and how, the lull would end. Each day, he studied the Intelligence reports and the situation summaries: these revealed an increase in action in the Isle of Wight area on 11 August, together with engagements off the Norfolk coast, and it seemed as if intensified air warfare was beginning to creep closer to his squadron.

Radar reported an upsurge in enemy activity soon after breakfast next morning, with Luftwaffe formations assembling over the French coast. Perowne handed this information to Lex, waiting to lead the first sortie; the section leader came near to faltering as he listened to Perowne. Only ten minutes later, the order to scramble sent Orange Section aloft, with Joe flying Number Two to Lex, and with Chris Treleaven completing the trio. Control instructed the Spitfires to locate an enemy force coming in towards Dungeness, which radar had picked up over the Channel; the raiders split just before the coast, one group heading west and the other east, and just before Dover, the Group Controller directed the Spitfires onto the second formation.

Treleaven located the 109s first, calling over the radio, 'Hello, Orange Leader. Bandits at 3 o'clock. Same Angels as us.'

Joe looked to his right and saw them immediately: eight aircraft, black against the cloud above them.

'I have them,' said Lex over the R/T. 'OK Orange Section. Let's get above them.'

The nose of the leading aircraft lifted and Joe climbed

113

after. Lex spoke again. 'They seem like 109s, but there's something queer about them.'

Joe examined the shapes more closely, and also noticed the difference to the normal 109 structure. Then Chris exclaimed, 'Jesus! They've got bombs under them!'

Treleaven was correct: the Luftwaffe fighters had been converted into bombers, with ugly-finned bombs slung beneath their bellies. Now, the enemy had increased speed, heading directly towards Dover, and making no attempt to turn up to the Spitfires in the normal defensive manner.

'OK, Orange Section,' called Lex. 'Here we go.' His aircraft slanted away to port, and Joe followed him down.

As the Spitfires approached the Germans in a long dive, Joe could see Dover. The enemy aircraft split as the section closed, still at maximum speed, and before Lex, Joe and Chris could reach them, the 109s were over the harbour and houses. They kept on, still outside range, towards the masts of the radar station beyond the town, and then Joe saw them starting to dive for bombing runs. By now, the gap had been cut to about 250 yards, and Joe watched the bullets begin to spray from Lex's aircraft – long, vicious bursts. Bombs exploded below, and smoke gushed from between the radar masts. But Lex's fire had hit one of the 109s before it could complete a turn, and Joe noticed part of its wing break away, with the aircraft swerving violently inland, Lex trying to keep on its tail. Joe continued to follow. Lex fired again, and smoke started to stream from the Messerschmitt's engine, but the German pilot still managed to wrench his crippled machine round towards Dover again.

'Damn it to hell!' shouted Lex. 'I'm out of bloody

114

ammunition. He'll have to be yours, Joe. Finish him off.' The Spitfire banked away, leaving the wounded German to Joe.

He knew the Messerschmitt to be incapable of escaping; the German pilot must have realized he could never have made it back across the Channel. Yet he still had his bomb, and he'd still to reach the sea, and beneath him lay farms and houses. Joe pushed forward the control column and dived. The strickened aircraft loomed in his sights, and smoke swirled back towards him. He closed to 200 yards. 'Bale out, bale out you fool,' he said to himself, but the German pilot stayed in his cockpit. Perhaps his canopy had jammed. Joe imagined him struggling to escape. Only 150 yards and he couldn't wait any longer. He pressed the button.

His Spitfire shook with the gun vibration. The enemy aircraft twisted almost vertical in a sudden convulsion before flipping into a slow, spiralling dive. Joe followed it down and could see the small figure of the pilot as the aircraft revolved. The Messerschmitt struck the beach just north of Dover, only a few feet from the sea. Joe flew in a tight circle above the black smoke, and saw people running along the beach: some stopped and waved up at him, no doubt considering him to be a hero. Joe knew the German pilot could have released his bomb over Dover, but instead had just tried to escape out to sea and home, despite the weight of the bomb dragging him down. Lex's voice sounded in Joe's cockpit. 'I reckon he's still mostly mine. But I'll share him with you. You can buy me a beer.'

The attack on Dover radar station, together with other bombing strikes on stations at Pevensey and Rye and even further west at Ventnor, was reported on the BBC one o'clock news as Susie washed up after lunch. All of

115

these were said to be new targets. 'None of the radar stations ceased operating,' said the announcer, 'and the damage is already being repaired. It is believed that the attacks may form part of a German plan to hinder Fighter Command defences prior to a major assault.'

Perowne led a second squadron sortie during the afternoon. Control warned that raiders were coming over the Channel in small batches; the Spitfires scrambled as quickly as possible, but the radar, damaged by the morning attacks, failed to give sufficient time to stop the enemy hitting Manston airfield. Manston seemed a fearful mess as Perowne flew over it, with one hangar completely wrecked and the airfield badly pock-marked. Then Control told him that Hawkinge was being hit, and he headed south-west at maximum speed. Radio traffic was noisier than usual. Once again, the Spitfires arrived too late. A third sortie led by Simon managed more success, with Womack downing a 109 and Taffy a 110; Treleaven had to bale out, but landed unhurt and he returned to the airfield within two hours.

George updated his theory, saying the Germans had started their big attempt – hitting the radar stations to blind Fighter Command, then the forward airfields along the coast like Manston and Hawkinge. The airfield at Lympne had also been bombed during the day. Once again, Perowne noted the reaction of his pilots: Simon, Lex and Taffy spent a noisy evening in the bar, their boredom ended; George and Womack discussed the latest situation in their normal, detached fashion; Perowne had seen Joe slip off to the farm again, and he remembered Simon's description of the girl – 'a real beauty – a bit young but who's bothered? A real filly – long legs and lovely movement and still unbroken. You should get your missus to paint her.' Perowne switched

116

off his light and lay on his side in the dark, trying to imagine the feel of Anna's body pressing against his back as they settled down to sleep.

An overcast, unsettled sky stretched over the farm, and the twins hurried through their breakfast and milking to follow their father down to the long meadow. The hay lay flat, cut the previous afternoon, and in the bare sections between the rows, Susie could see the faint ruts where Joe's Spitfire had landed. The twins began to rake, working next to one another and moving sideways across the field towards the beeches. Only a few minutes later, a formation of aircraft curved down from the low cloud, diving northwards.

Peter looked up. 'Spitfires!' he shouted. Susie watched them disappear beyond the Downs towards Chatham. 'They seem in an almighty hurry,' said her brother. 'Something must be happening – listen!' The sound came again – a harsh, ripping noise. 'Browning machine-guns!' exclaimed Peter. With the fire from the weapons, came a rising and falling hum of engines, gradually fading. Then more aircraft appeared from the cloud: two formations following one another to disappear westwards. Susie began to rake the grass again, her hands unsteady on the smooth wooden shaft, and she tried to ignore Peter's excited chatter.

By the time the dispersal telephone rang at 7.45, Lex's hands were shaking so much that he could barely light a cigarette, and the ringing of the instrument on the wall kicked him like a blow in the stomach. He picked up the receiver; Womack was already turning from the chess game which he'd been playing on his own in the corner; Joe had tossed aside his book. Within seven minutes, Lex was leading his section westwards. Apparently,

German bombers had come north off Ramsgate, then turned into the Thames Estuary under cloud cover; they were thought to be aiming for the Sheerness and Chatham area. Hurricanes coming down from North Weald clashed with the enemy near the North Foreland, with Lex hearing the dogfights over the R/T.

Then Control came through. 'Hello, Piper Orange Leader. Steer 090 degrees – zero nine zero. Climb to Angels X for X-Ray.' Lex acknowledged and altered course, climbing to 20,000 feet and searching from side to side with the usual restless wing movements, and all the time, his stomach muscles were tensed like steel hoops. Then he saw them through the murk, just below – three, four, then about five more bombers emerging one by one. Dorniers.

'Tallyho!' he shouted. He dived, and tracer immediately spat up from the German rear gunners. He fired almost blindly, as if trying to use his own bullets to block those curving up towards him, and the enemy cannon fire seemed bound to hit him, until the lines bent away at the last moment. His section closed. The Dorniers broke formation, trying to get back into cloud. He fired again, and again he missed, so he banked to make another attempt. He saw Womack diving on a Dornier, and in a second, the enemy aircraft was a blazing wreck, dropping through the hole in the clouds.

Above, another Dornier banked, flying at full throttle in a desperate effort to reach cover, and Lex's strained mouth twisted into a grin: his Spitfire was in a perfect attack position. He climbed at maximum speed and opened fire at 250 yards; he could see his bullets flickering along the Dornier's fuselage. But the bomber continued to slant towards the clouds; he fired again and could see the bullets hit, yet the bomber still went on. The cloud swirled around it and he followed. Visibility was nil; he pushed forward the stick, and dived below the layer, looking frantically to port and starboard yet still seeing no sign of his victim. He circled twice, anger and desperation temporarily replacing his fear. The enemy had disappeared. He could see smoke rising further west: the Germans must have unloaded their bombs as fast as they could, then headed for home.

He saw another Spitfire in the distance and joined up with him, recognising Joe's number. They came back to base together, seeing nothing, and for a moment, Lex felt the warmth of relief seep into him overcoming his frustration at not obtaining a definite kill: for a few minutes, it was all over, and he would be reprieved for another hour or so while his Spitfire was rearmed and refuelled, and while he waited for the telephone to ring again.

Womack was missing for sixty minutes, until Lex heard he'd come down safely at Biggin Hill. The squadron also learnt that the Luftwaffe had attempted early-morning raids at Eastchurch on Sheppey, and in the west at Bognor and Portland, even though weather conditions were difficult over the Channel. Now, the forecasters declared brighter weather would arrive before the afternoon. Lex sat in his chair near the telephone. Chris Treleaven arrived to replace Womack, and continued the chess game in the corner; Joe took up the book which he'd been reading, and his dog settled beside his chair. Lex's fear built up inside him once more.

Clouds remained above the meadow, and the twins were chivvied on by their father to rake the hay into stoops as soon as possible. The thick foliage in the wood shivered with the uneasy wind, but the air stayed warm and close, and Susie's thin blouse stuck to her skin as she worked. They ate a rushed lunch by the rising stoops,

Susie rubbing her aching arms and feeling the blisters on the palms of her hands. Denied the BBC news, they were ignorant of events in the air battle so near to them: aircraft had flown above the farm throughout the morning, invisible in the lowering clouds; once the twins heard deep explosions from the north, six or more in rapid succession.

Joe repeatedly glanced at the clock. Over three hours had passed. He'd managed to complete five or six pages of his book, but the words remained incomprehensible, despite his constant re-reading of the same paragraphs. Mops stayed by him. All the time, each of those 200 minutes, he expected the sudden ring of the telephone to pierce the silence. It came just before noon. He watched Lex's face as he lifted the receiver, and the section leader seemed to grimace slightly as he listened. 'OK – understood,' he said. Joe and Chris were already on their feet, and pushing through the chairs to the door.

The section was ordered to intercept raiders near Chatham, and the Spitfires made for the area at full throttle – only to find the enemy had been blocked further east. For a moment, Joe thought they might be allowed to return home; instead, the section was moved south-west to patrol the Canterbury area.

Chris's voice sounded soon after the Spitfires had banked towards the new patrol line. 'Hello, Orange Leader. My engine's giving out. I'll have to leave you.'

Lex replied, 'OK, Orange Three. See you later. Set up the beers.' Joe watched Chris's aircraft peel away to starboard, and wished it were him. But just two minutes later, Chris's voice came again. 'Orange Three here. Bandits, bandits. Am being attacked.' A moment later, he spoke once more. 'I am alone. Please help me. I am alone.' Joe expected to see Lex alter direction, and he didn't know whether he felt relief or guilt when the section leader continued to fly according to his orders. Chris didn't speak again.

Lex and Joe suddenly broke from the thin mist into glaring sunshine. Beneath them, the tumbled sun-starched cloud spread out beyond Kent to the sea, and the sky arched blue and pure. Joe felt immediate fear that the enemy might be lurking up in the sun, and he squinted upwards through the shimmering perspex as the two Spitfires flew on. The aircraft rose and fell gently on the air currents, and over the radio Joe could hear the fighting elsewhere: heavy engagements were apparently taking place over the Thames Estuary, and the jumble of radio communications continued to fill the air as Joe and Lex flew across the empty sky.

'Hello, Piper Orange Leader.' Control was calling. 'Bandits approaching your location course south-west eighty degrees, zero, eight, zero. Approximately 30 Do 17s very scattered heading for coastal exit. Peter Squadron already in contact. Move to assist. Good hunting.'

Lex immediately banked and the two Spitfires searched for the Dorniers, which should be coming into view as they tried to escape from the 56 Squadron Hurricanes. Within moments, Joe saw them, five thousand feet below: the German bombers were trying to bunch together, and to force a way through the swarming Hurricanes, back into the cloud.

Once again, Joe followed Lex into the dive. He hunched himself over the stick; his breath came in quick jerks, and the dogfights surged larger as his Spitfire carried him down. Once more, he felt her shudder as her guns began to fire, and suddenly the sky was full of whirling, jerking, rushing black shapes.

Susie and Peter stood in the yard. They didn't feel the weight of the milk buckets heavy in their hands. Above them, the noise had suddenly become deafening, with machine--gun fire clattering down to them above the protesting moan and roar of overworked aircraft engines. Susie could see nothing: she stood with her face upturned towards the clouds, her lips nipped tight between her teeth, and Nellie whined at her heels. A sudden tinkling sounded from the far side of the yard, and Susie saw dozens of small, bright objects rolling from the barn slates and bouncing onto the cobbles. Peter had already slopped down his bucket and was running towards them; he rushed back with one in his hand. 'Look!' he exclaimed, thrusting the object into Susie's reluctant fingers. 'It's a shell-case.' Susie felt it still warm in her palm, and above her, the dreadful din continued, rising and falling.

Joe fought in a frenzy, his finger stabbing the button in burst after burst, desperately trying to avoid being hit in the terrible cross-fire, and to avoid colliding with other aircraft. Outside his cockpit whirled a picture of three-dimensional hell with the aircraft screwing and twisting, and he couldn't look in enough directions fast enough; he trusted in his Spitfire to weave a way through.

Suddenly, he reached safe sky. Somehow, he had dived through the dogfights, levelled, and climbed again without remembering any detailed manoeuvring. Now, the sun burnt sharp on his face. He steadied his Spitfire and tipped her forward again, and there below was the mess of aircraft. He knew he could leave them, or plunge into it all again, and temptation almost made him flee for home. He made himself push the stick forward, and his Spitfire responded. He whispered, 'Come on – take us through it again,' and the aircraft hurtled downwards.

Ahead, he could see a lumbering Dornier. He came closer and could see the German rear-gunner in his turret, swerving his weapon round and upwards. Bullets from Joe's Spitfire sprayed to one side of the bomber; he altered deflection. Then the German gunner fired. Cannon and incendiary bullets floated lazily upwards, and the Spitfire lurched as if trying to shake herself away. The perspex above Joe's head suddenly crazed in a giant jig-saw pattern; a heavy metallic snap sounded beneath his feet, and oil gushed in front of his eyes. His Spitfire twisted to starboard, with clouds, aircraft, vivid blue sky and sun revolving faster and faster around his head. Mist covered him like a shroud and Joe plunged helplessly toward the earth.

'Look!' shouted Peter. Susie had already seen it, and stood with eyes wide with shock. The aircraft had burst from beneath the cloud almost above their heads. It spiralled down, flames leaping from its engine, and filthy smoke smearing the sky behind. The aircraft began to spin faster and faster with a rising screech, and then the engine seemed to explode and the wreckage of the fighter fell silently. Suddenly, something was thrown out to one side, falling with the aircraft until a splash of white began to stream behind. But the pilot's parachute failed to open fully. It streaked after him, half-catching the wind, and Susie could see the man being twisted and twirled as he dropped.

Peter was already running. Both of them ran across the yard, through the gate and down the lane. In front of them, the aircraft had plunged into the wood beyond the bottom orchard, with a massive rush of smoke and flames sprouting from the trees. Susie heard the roar of the explosion above her sucking breath as she clambered over the fence and into the orchard; she ran between the apple-trees, ducking beneath the branches, her breath coming in sharper sobs; brambles snagged her skirt and scratched her thighs as she scrambled out into the beech wood. She could hear the crackling of machine-gun bullets in the burning aircraft.

'Over here!' called Peter. 'I think he's over here!' He stopped to look for a moment beneath the trees, and Susie caught up with him; then, they were running again. They saw the remains of the parachute – tattered long strips hanging very white from the beech branches – and beneath, among the carpet of rotting red leaves, lay the man. They reached him together. Susie threw herself down on her knees beside him, and she saw the yellow-white face, the open twisted mouth frozen in a fearful smile, and the curls sodden with blood. She knelt beside him as if praying, then suddenly leant forward with her hands covering her face and her long hair almost touching his cheeks, her fingers wet with tears of relief because he wasn't Joe.

Peter almost pushed her aside as he bent to put his head to the pilot's chest. 'He's still alive!'

Susie whispered, 'He's not Joe.'

'Of course he isn't! Don't be so bloody silly – we must get help. We'd better not move him. He must be hurt inside – and look at his legs!'

The pilot's legs were wrenched into violent angles, and just above the right ankle, where the cloth was soaked dark with blood, Susie saw the white of bone. She could smell burning – one of his arms had been blackened by fire. 'We must get help,' Peter repeated. 'I'll go. I'll telephone from home – Dad may come – he must've seen the aircraft falling. You stay – will you be all right?' She nodded, and he left her with the pilot.

124

Joe felt no fear as his aircraft fell. Just the certainty of death. All terror had gone, washed away by the sure knowledge that he was dying. No more sapping numbing terror, no more fear of wounds and mutilation and fire. It had come as he always knew it would, as they all knew it would for each of them, and he let his Spitfire take him down, spinning towards the inevitable end.

Yet she didn't want to die or Joe to die, and she saved them both. They whirled together in the cloud, tossing and jerking with the streams of white tangled around them, and Joe couldn't tell whether he was falling or rising, but then they broke through, and she'd dropped into a long and gentle dive, with the fields and farms sliding smoothly below. And even while her black blood still washed around Joe's feet and splashed warm on his face, her heart began to beat again. The engine throbbed and burst into an uneven, labouring pulse; the stick in Joe's hands trembled and tugged his fingers, and she answered when he slowly moved the column back. She levelled and they flew together again.

She brought him all the way home to safety, with Joe scarcely conscious of the direction; they curved down gradually to the airfield, and her wheels touched the earth, shaky but sufficiently sure. He sat trembling in the cockpit. The hood slid back, and hands helped him out, then Joe broke free and he went back to her, smoothing his fingers gently over the skin of her wing to feel the wounds. He heard Simon's voice. He let them guide him away, and Mops came jumping out to meet him. Only then did he feel the pain in his thigh, as if someone were shredding his skin with a red-hot saw, and he sagged to the grass with Mops whimpering beside him.

CHAPTER ELEVEN

Susie still knelt by the pilot. She became aware of the crackling flames from further into the wood where the aircraft had crashed, and the sickly smell of burning rubber drifted across the clearing. A thrush, frightened from the undergrowth by the explosion, returned to the bushes, and the remains of the parachute swung gently above her head.

The pilot moved. His eyes were still shut, and as he shifted his head, Susie could see the wound behind the right ear. Sticking to the glistening gash were leaves from the carpet under the tree, and Susie moved round behind the boy, still on her knees, slowly lifting his head to rest it in her lap. He made no sound. She crouched there, his head heavy on her thighs, with his blood seeping through to her skin, and nearby the thrush began to sing again. Susie looked down into the pilot's face. He suddenly opened his eyes. They were blue, and as she looked into them, Susie could see the tiny specks of grey. She didn't know if the stranger could see or hear her, and she found herself whispering again and again, 'Joe, Joe, Joe.'

Gradually, the flecks of grey faded and the blue became opaque. Susie felt Peter crouch beside her and she said, 'He's dead.' His head still rested on her lap. Faint sunshine broke through the branches above them, and as the thin rays struck down through the quivering leaves, they lit the boy's face and lips and seemed to make them tremble, as if he were about to cry or smile.

Perowne listened to the BBC news with Simon standing

next to him at the bar. The announcer revealed that engagements had taken place throughout Kent and Sussex during the day; airfields had been the main target. 'Thirteen RAF aircraft are reported lost, but ten of the pilots are said to be safe. German losses total at least 78 machines destroyed for certain, with a further 33 probables and 49 damaged. It is clear that the enemy is failing in the bid to cripple the effectiveness of Fighter Command, and the extent of the losses must be causing serious concern to the German High Command.'

The wireless began to play light music. Perowne counted again the casualties inflicted by his own squadron during the day; Lex had returned from his last sortie with another bomber to his credit – this, added to others obtained by Simon, Taffy and himself, plus Joe's 109 which Lex claimed a one-half share, gave a total of six. In return, Chris had gone and Joe lay in hospital. Perowne looked around him: Lex was slumped fast asleep in an armchair; George and Womack were playing another of their interminable games of chess. Taffy and Henny were down at the pub. The mess seemed empty and too quiet – and Perowne had only seven pilots left for duty.

'Joe seemed pretty shaken,' he said to Simon.

'He'll soon buck up again.'

'I'm not so sure. His leg may soon heal but his nerves may be bad. I don't know how he managed to get back.'

'Bloody good flying. A rest for a day or so will work wonders. He seemed more cheerful tonight. Get him to stay at the farm – Susie'll nurse him.' Simon added, 'Wish it were me.'

Next day, the clouds began to lift by mid-morning. Perowne had already led one patrol before breakfast, without contact. Then the Met reports indicated a fine spell,

Intelligence believed the Germans would increase their attempts against airfields, and orders came through to Perowne for additional patrols along the south coast. The whole squadron went up this time in two sections, with Perowne leading the first, comprising four aircraft, and Lex weaving behind with the remaining three. The Spitfires patrolled the sector just inland from Rye, spreading over towards the forward airfield at Lympne. Not long after the sections had taken up position, Control reported radar contact with 50-plus raiders approaching from the Calais area; Perowne turned south to attempt interception before they crossed the coast.

The squadron failed to contact the raiders: broken cloud still hindered visibility and Control misdirected the Spitfires too far south. The Germans apparently slipped above, and came in around Dungeness, turning north towards Lympne and Hawkinge, and Perowne's squadron was still searching just off the coast when the R/T reported Lympne and Hawkinge being heavily attacked by the dive-bombers, especially Lympne. Perowne chased after the departing raiders, ordering his pilots to boost engines, but pursuit proved hopeless: the Squadron-Leader noted the dwindling fuel level, and took the section down lower for the flight back, breaking cloud just before the coast.

As the aircraft emerged into the clear sky, he glanced at his section. Immediately, he noted the untidy appearance of the two Spitfires to his right – they were flying much too close together.

'Hello, Yellow Three. Watch your distance.' Perowne waited for Taffy, at the end of the line, to respond by moving out: the Welshman's aircraft continued to shift closer to Womack. Perhaps Taffy's R/T had failed. He spoke over the radio again. 'Hello, Yellow Two. Give Taffy more room.'

128

At that moment, the Spitfires touched. Perowne stared horrified as the two aircraft suddenly flicked into one another, crashed together, reared skywards, then rolled and started to spin still locked tight. The R/T remained silent. The coupled aircraft plunged into the sea in one huge eruption of spray, and sank immediately. Perowne circled above, but could see nothing except the widening smear of oil on the water, and the sickening sight stayed with him as he led the remains of his squadron back to the airfield: Taffy, so confident, Womack, so careful – perhaps the tragedy came from sheer weariness, perhaps from over-eagerness to search the sky for Stukas. Perowne realized he had five pilots left until replacements could arrive and Joe could return, and the Luftwaffe's main offensive had clearly begun.

Raiders struck again at Kent again in the early afternoon, strike after strike with small groups harrying from one direction after another. Orange Section went up – George and Henny with Lex leading. The three Spitfires were still aloft when the enemy bombers reached the squadron airfield. Perowne only received minimum warning. Hurricanes from 111 Squadron tried to intercept, but the 110s and bomb-carrying 109s broke through the screen, circled northwards, and began their runs.

Perowne was in the dispersal hut. Bombs began to explode at the far end of the field, erupting towards him. The ground shook, and the windows in the hut rattled with increasing violence. Men were running towards the hangars in an attempt to close the bomb-blast doors, and Perowne sprinted across the grass to join them. Two more Messerschmitts dived to deliver their loads. A bomb landed amongst the trainer aircraft parked by the side of the buildings, and they began to explode, one after another; the blast of the second bomb buffetted into Perowne, and almost threw him down, but he kept on running towards the gaping entrance to the hangar. He could see a mechanic struggling to close the heavy doors. And then, he felt himself being lifted and hurled sideways; he rolled onto his back, and could see the Messerschmitt curving upwards again, and another coming down behind it.

He heard a shrill bark. Joe's dog was running in a panic across the grass, seeking her absent master. 'Mops!' he shouted. 'Here, girl! Here!' The dog veered towards the sound of his voice. Behind her, the Messerschmitt's machine-guns began to fire, Perowne shouted again. The puppy came running to him, whimpering, and he clutched the long thick hair on her back. As he crouched there on his knees holding her, he could see the machine-gun bullets spurting along the soil towards him. They missed him by barely a yard. The aircraft roared just above his head with the stench of its over-heated engine spreading over him, and the bullets stitched onwards towards the hangar. The mechanic had just managed to slam the doors together when the bullets killed him: he flung up his arms and slid to the ground as the machine-gun fire sprayed on over the side of the hangar and along the roof. Perowne felt the dog's licks still wet on his face as he watched the enemy aircraft bank southwards, and Hurricanes curved in to chase them away.

Simon took Joe to the farm early next morning, half-carrying him upstairs to the spare room at the front of the house, with Mops padding behind; then he hurried out again, saying to Susie, 'Can't stay, love. These clouds are expected to lift. Looks as if it's going to be busy again.' Peter was still at the market with his father, and after Simon's car had roared down the track, Susie was alone for a moment with Joe. Her mother called upstairs, 'Don't be too long. That poor boy wants plenty of sleep.'

He smiled up at her, his face grey against the fresh whiteness of the pillow. The weak sunlight made his skin seem even more pallid, then the clouds dropped again to smudge the sharpness of his cheek-bones. 'I shouldn't really be here.'

'Of course you should.'

'It was Simon's idea and the CO agreed. They've both been grand.' He reached up and held her hand, and Susie closed her fingers around his for a moment to warm them. He said, 'I can't believe I'm here.'

Her mother called again and Susie left him. Mops stayed curled up by the side of his bed, her tail flopping slowly in lazy contentment. Later, Susie found them both asleep. Outside the clouds had lifted, and the BBC news reported fresh Luftwaffe attacks against airfields on the south coast, followed by strikes in the north-east.

Soon after 2 pm, enemy aircraft were detected approaching Essex, Suffolk and North Kent. Interception was rendered even more difficult by the scattered nature of the attacks. Perowne, flying with his sections in the Canterbury area, listened to the confused babble over the R/T, and guessed that Hurricanes were heavily engaged somewhere near Harwich; then Control instructed his Spitfires to block a large force of bombers and fighters believed to be approaching the north Kent area. He immediately banked northwards. With him flew the entire squadron strength: Lex, Simon, George, Henny and two newcomers who had arrived together only 90 minutes before the Spitfires scrambled – Sergeant Peres and Pilot Officer Chapman.

Three minutes later, the Spitfires joined with Hurricanes also heading for the threatened area; almost immediately, the enemy formations were located close to the Thames Estuary. Perowne and his pilots had no time to reach the Dorniers before escorting Messerschmitt fighters dived to protect them, and even while Perowne's aircraft twisted and turned in the dogfights, he could hear Control frantically calling for other squadrons to block the bombers, now attacking airfields at Rochester, Eastchurch and Hawkinge.

Fifteen minutes later, Perowne circled his own airfield to see fresh bomb craters around the buildings. With him landed George and Sergeant Peres; Lex and Henny arrived while he walked towards dispersal. An orderly informed him that the other newcomer, Chapman, had landed at Detling. Only Simon was still missing. Perowne sagged into a chair; outside the ground crews were already refuelling and rearming the aircraft for the next sortie. The telephone rang. For a moment, Perowne thought the message must be another scramble order: instead the airfield control tower told him that Simon was approaching, with his Spitfire badly damaged.

He sprinted across the grass and into the Control Room. Simon's aircraft was circling to the south. He grabbed a pair of glasses, focused, and found him, and as the Spitfire came nearer, he could see one wheel hanging: the Spitfire's undercarriage had been hit, and the other wheel torn off. He knew that to land like that would be virtual suicide – one wheel would never provide sufficient support when the aircraft touched the ground.

Simon's voice broke over the radio into the Control Room, calm and clear and seeming only a few feet away. 'Hello, Piper Control. Piper Orange Two calling. Will you clear the landing area, please? Out.'

Spitfires were already being shifted from the centre of the airfield. Perowne sat in front of the R/T set.

'Hello, Simon. Simon, this is Teddy.'

'Hello, old man.'

'Simon, your starboard leg is dangling. Can't you get it up?' No wheels would be better than one.

'No. The blasted thing is jammed.'

'Then bale out.'

'Negative. The hood's KO.'

'Try it again.'

A pause, then Simon repeated, 'Negative.' The Spitfire circled again and Perowne attempted desperately to think of something to say. He watched Simon bank, dive suddenly, flick into another climb, fly low over the airfield violently waggling his wings, all in a vain effort to unstick the starboard leg, and as he flew close to the Control Tower, he could see Simon's shape in the cockpit.

'Simon. Try the cover again. You must bale out.'

'Can't. It won't let me go.'

The fire-engines and ambulance were already waiting at the far end of the airfield. Simon spoke again, for the last time. 'I'm coming in. Christ I could do with a drink. Get one ready for me Teddy, and this one's on me. See you in a minute. Cheerio – I'm switching off.'

The radio died. Perowne could imagine Simon going through all the emergency procedures: radio off, seat harness tightened, seat lowered to protect his head in case the aircraft turned over, parachute released, oxygen tube unfastened. Yet the hood still trapped him like a coffin lid, even though he could see safety just a few yards away. The Spitfire turned slowly beyond the airfield, dropping lower and growing steadily larger as it approached. Simon levelled, and the bright disc of the whirling propeller disappeared as he cut the engine. Perowne noticed that the approach was perfect; the fire tenders and ambulance followed the Spitfire, as Simon glided those few precious feet from the ground.

The solitary wheel touched, and immediately snapped under the weight. The aircraft collapsed shatteringly onto its belly. It slid with an agonized scraping scream, the propeller buckled, the starboard wing gouging into the earth, and then it began to spin, each time faster, before the port wing rose and the whole aircraft rose as if about to flip onto its back. Instead, it pivoted on the starboard wing, almost slowly it seemed, then slid to the ground as the wing broke beneath the strain. Immediately a sheet of flame jumped high from the wreckage, scorching above the oily smoke.

For a moment Perowne couldn't move. The fire tenders had screeched to a stop only yards from the flames, and the high pressure hoses were already spraying foam onto the fire; smoke gushed blacker and thicker, and men were disappearing into it. Perowne saw them dragging something out – Simon.

He clambered down the wooden stairs and ran across the field, and even from fifty yards he could feel the heat from the Spitfire burning his throat. He pushed aside the medical orderly who was just shutting the ambulance door. Simon's charred flesh looked filthy black against the grey RAF blankets. Only his face was visible. None of the features were recognizable – just the open slit of the mouth, the startling white of the teeth, and the clean pink of his tongue. Around his neck hung the remains of the pink silk scarf. The orderly slammed the door, slapped his palm against the rear of the ambulance, and the vehicle accelerated away.

Simon was still breathing when they reached the hospital. Perowne heard this news, and no more, in the last minutes before the telephone shrieked in the dispersal hut, and he ran once again to his Spitfire. Fresh waves of raiders were crossing the Kent coast near Dungeness;

heavy attacks had already been launched further west in the Portland area, and it seemed the Luftwaffe would never cease their attempt to batter Fighter Command airfields – attempts which were so often proving successful. And as Perowne headed south with his six remaining Spitfires, he realized that of the squadron pilots who had flown with him at the time of Dunkirk, only Lex and George remained in action. And Joe would have to be told about Simon.

Susie sat by the window, stroking Mops and looking out over the fields: she could hear her mother bustling in the kitchen below, Peter whistling while he worked in the barn, and the gentle sound of Joe's breathing as he slept. She turned to watch his face. Some of the greyness had faded; his lips were slightly parted as if he were about to smile, and they reminded her of the dying pilot in the woods. She felt a faint wave of sickness, and she wanted Joe to move and come alive.

His eyes opened and he looked straight at her, but she said nothing, and his eyes closed again; she'd never realized before how long were his lashes. Then, he looked at her once more and smiled. 'I thought I must still be dreaming.'

'I was trying not to wake you. You looked so peaceful. How does your leg feel?'

'Much better. It was only a flesh wound – it's a bit sore but it'll do. Soon I shall feel a fraud lying here.'

Perowne half-rolled to lose the 109 on his tail. Then suddenly, he saw the Dornier ahead of him, and he pulled the boost control to close on the enemy bomber, feeling his Spitfire vibrating as it responded to give maximum power. He manoeuvred into position, and found he was travelling much too fast; he throttled back, swung up, took aim and fired. Almost at once, he saw the tiny flashes of fire sparkling along the Dornier fuselage. He closed in again, when suddenly the bomber reared; he heaved at the controls to prevent a collision, and in doing so, lost sight of the enemy for a moment; when he banked, he saw the Dornier going down below him with smoke pouring from its centre section. He dived, dropping from 20,000 feet to only 3,000 feet at such a speed that the bottom panel of the Spitfire cracked, and his ears roared with the sudden change of pressure. Just as he closed again, the Dornier jinked into a steep, climbing turn. He fired and the multitude of lights once more flickered along the hull, almost instantaneously swallowed by a burst of flames. With that the Dornier twisted gently earthwards.

As he flew back to the airfield, his weariness washed out all consciousness of direction or behaviour. He heard dimly over the R/T that further airfields had been attacked. And Luftwaffe bombers had reached Croydon, in the London suburbs: it seemed that the capital would now become a target. He remembered Anna's pleading voice over the telephone the previous night, begging him to see her. Did she want him or just his body? In his tiredness, Perowne no longer knew or cared; he just wanted her safe, yet no matter how many bombers his pilots brought down, more seemed to follow, flooding over the Channel to batter the airfields upon which Fighter Command relied.

Somehow, he found himself above his own base, and he shook aside his exhaustion for a moment to bring his Spitfire down among the bomb craters.

Next morning the Fighter Command Intelligence Report declared, 'Recent activities of the GAF suggest the opening phase in an attempt to gain air superiority by a process of exhausting attacks on fighter defences. . . . On the 11th, 12th, 13th and 14th August, approximately 50 per cent of the total German strength of dive-bombers and fighters was probably employed, together with about 15 per cent of the long-range bomber force.' Perowne sat with the paper on the desk in front of him; his eyes still felt heavy despite the drugged sleep into which he'd dropped the previous evening. Outside the clouds sagged low, but the weather was expected to clear by noon. He wondered if he might have time to hurry to the farm and see Joe, to break the news about Simon; he felt tempted to telephone instead. He decided to wait a few more hours: according to the hospital, Simon was still alive, yet might go at any moment.

Someone knocked gently on his door. A young pilot entered, and Perowne stood to welcome him. He couldn't even remember the replacement's name. 'Philip Brookes sir.' The boy appeared about twenty; his face was flushed with shyness, his hazel eyes anxious to please, his palm damp with nervousness as he shook hands.

'How many flying hours have you done, Philip?'

'About 170 sir.'

'And how many in Spitfires?'

'Fifteen, sir.'

Perowne grimaced as he turned away: only fifteen – the boy would be lucky if he survived another five. The squadron operational strength now stood at seven pilots, but only on paper; and the worst might still be to come.

Clouds had still to lift by the time his first section scrambled at 1.15, with Lex leading Henny and Chapman to join Hurricanes attempting to block fresh raids into Kent. Perowne followed an hour later with George and Peres. By now, the sun had broken through, although wisps of cirrus still hung at 20,000 feet to provide protection for enemy fighters escorting the Luftwaffe bombers.

Susie sat beside Joe on the bank of the Medway. She could hear the sound of her father's van dwindling in the distance, and she felt suddenly shy again, wishing the afternoon were over, and that her mother had never suggested Joe should be taken to sit by the river. Joe seemed even more of a stranger in this place where she'd been so often to swim with Peter. In front, the water stretched wide and smooth, thirty yards across to the deep brown shadows beneath the overhanging elms; to their left, the reeds grew thick to the river's edge, and Mops was floundering among them following strange scents.

Joe broke the silence. 'I used to like swimming.' Then suddenly, he started to tell Susie about himself, and his decision both surprised and pleased her. He talked slowly and quietly, and he hardly looked at Susie. He was country born, as much as she; his mother was dead; a younger brother had drowned in a sailing accident two years before. 'Peter reminds me of him. Perhaps that's why I feel so easy with him.' Until he joined the RAF, he'd lived alone with his father, a rural vet. 'We get on extraordinarily well. You'd like him, Susie. He's quiet, like you – keeps very much to himself.' Joe's home was a small cottage deep in the Lake District, near Langdale, beneath the shadow of the mountains, with the pine woods surging down the slope to the rear of the house, and as Joe spoke Susie could sense the loneliness in his voice.

He stopped abruptly. 'I'm sorry, Susie. I shouldn't have gone on so long.'

'I'd like to hear more.'

'It's good to talk.' He lay back against the grass, his

138

eyes closed. Susie waited for him to speak again, but he remained silent. She sat still, watching the midges circling just above the water in front of her. The sun had broken through the thin cloud veil and struck warm on her legs; the light slanted down into the water and wavered the shadows of the pebbles. Joe seemed asleep. Susie walked along the bank, with the grass soft beneath her bare feet, until she reached the sandy stretch where she'd picnicked with Peter in the past; she waded into the water and lifted her skirt as the current pushed against her calves then over the backs of her knees. She made her way slowly upriver, skirt held high, carefully placing each foot between the slippery stones, and as she looked down she could see the reflection of her sunburnt legs in the water. She glanced at Joe again. Now, he was leaning on his elbow, watching her, his face serious. She smiled at him, pulling back the hair from her eyes with one hand, and the skirt still bunched high in the other. She no longer felt shy. She waded towards him, and sat beside him on the bank again, tucking up her skirt above her wet thighs.

In the silence she heard an aircraft, then another. Further along the bank, Mops had begun to whine.

'Spitfire,' said Joe. 'And I think the other's a Messerschmitt. Yes, over there, see?'

Susie could see them: two silver dots high to the north, weaving steadily southwards in front of them, rising and falling and circling like midges. Now Susie heard the faint bursts of gunfire. Each time, she expected to see one aircraft explode into flames, and she couldn't tell which was the British and which the German, nor did it seem to matter. The dogfight moved slowly across the sky, then one aircraft suddenly broke away, diving southwards with the other turning into the chase.

'Probably no ammunition left,' muttered Joe. 'Or running low on fuel. Poor beggar. I don't think he'll make it.' Susie still didn't know the nationality of the victor. The aircraft disappeared, and the silence settled again, this time uneasy. Susie, still sitting up, suddenly noticed the faint scratches on her thighs, where the brambles had snagged her as she'd run to the pilot in the woods.

'It's our birthday tomorrow.' Susie had hardly meant to speak. 'Peter and I are eighteen.'

Joe turned to look at her. 'Why didn't you tell me before?' Then his smile faded. 'But I won't be able to get anything for you. Wait a minute – now where was it? Yes, I'll give you a present now. Close your eyes tight – no cheating. You'd better kneel – I can't reach properly with this dratted leg. Don't open your eyes.'

Susie knelt, smiling, her eyes still closed. She felt his hand lightly on her neck, then her hair being lifted and something brushing against her breast. 'You can open your eyes.' She looked down and saw the necklace: a bright polished pebble, amber coloured with tinges of purple, and with a hole washed by the river through the centre into which Joe had threaded his shoelace. 'The string is a bit clumsy,' he grinned, 'but it's the best I can manage.' 'I think it's lovely.' Susie noticed his hands were trembling close to her breast as he straightened the stone.

They lay in the sun again, and after a while, he slept. She fingered the pebble, feeling the smoothness of the stone, and she turned her head to look at his face. His arm rested against her side. Susie knew Joe was part of her, and she wouldn't want it otherwise, in spite of the fear. There would be no escape, and no release from the daily fear for either of them, until all was over, one way or the other. Mops barked, and Susie heard the sound of

140

the van. She sat up and placed the pebble inside her blouse between her breasts; the sun had warmed the stone, and now her own body would retain that warmth. She bent and gently woke him, and as she did so, the moan of aircraft sounded once more from the north.

CHAPTER TWELVE

For just under five minutes, Lex believed he'd conquered his fear. During those minutes, the dogfight tossed above the Medway Towns, and Lex knew he outclassed his lone opponent and eventually he would kill; it was only a matter of time. Twice, he almost succeeded, as the German pilot committed momentary errors; each time, Lex's bullets hit the 109. He felt calm and strangely relaxed, even though sweat saturated his clothing, and cramp knifed into his calves. Now he closed again with the Messerschmitt jigging in his sights; he dropped slightly below the enemy plane and, at that moment, the German pilot sloped into a dive. Then, as Lex pressed the button, he knew the fight was over. His bullets caught the 109's belly, raking the length of the fuselage and almost severing the tail. The Messerschmitt somersaulted, the tail section broke away, and the remains plunged vertically to the Thames Estuary 9,000 feet below. Lex waited to see if a parachute opened, but none appeared, so he altered course for home elated with his triumph.

Then reaction began. Perhaps the German pilot had merely been incompetent, rather than he himself being skilled; perhaps the German pilot had been even more tired; perhaps the Messerschmitt had suffered from a mechanical defect. And a triumph today would do nothing to prevent his own death, the next day or the next. Fear swamped back again. Lex approached his airfield, and smoke rose from the trees to tell him of a fresh raid, even before he sighted the devastation: new craters had been punched into the landing area, buildings were blazing, men and vehicles were rushing in apparent panic. The R/T crackled in the Spitfire cockpit. 'Hello, Orange Leader. Piper field inoperative. Divert to Apple. Repeat Apple.' He altered course to the next airfield, and the destruction of his own squadron base served to increase his insecurity.

Perowne walked among the ruins of the squadron home, smoke stinging his eyes, and his boots crunching on broken glass. The four bombers had disappeared less than six minutes before his return from the sortie. He tried to estimate the damage; three hangars were completely destroyed, together with the majority of stores buildings and the pumping station. The Salvation Army hut tilted at an insane angle. The cookhouse had half-collapsed, and a huge pool of water steadily lapped across the gravel, on which floated splintered planks, pots, and sodden packing cases. Nearby, medical orderlies were tending to a group of bewildered wounded.

Yet the control tower remained operative; the main mess still stood; working parties were already filling the craters through which Perowne and George had managed to thread a landing path, and their Spitfires were being refuelled and rearmed. Perowne knew Lex, Henny and the newcomer Brookes to be safe at the neighbouring airfield, and Chapman at Biggin Hill. Only Peres had to be accounted for. With luck, the airfield should be working again by the morning, and the squadron gathered together once more. But for how long? The airfield had already suffered four bombing raids in the last forty-eight hours; Intelligence Reports revealed even greater damage inflicted on other bases, and the same assessments spoke of the likelihood of continued Luftwaffe attempts to destroy Fighter Command, both in the sky and on the ground. As George had just said, his voice maddeningly calm and detached as always, 'They've only to keep this up, and they'll get their command of the air.'

Perowne felt too tired to think beyond the next few hours. He turned from the wreckage, and walked into the office, where he swept the shattered glass from his desk and picked up the telephone to find latest news of Simon. The instrument still worked. Weariness buffeted into him as he listened to the clipped words of the nurse. Simon would survive, although his face was likely to be heavily disfigured. No, he would never fly again. He might not even walk.

The telephone rang only a few moments later. He rubbed his eyes with his filthy, sweat-stained fingers, lifted the receiver, and allowed Anna's warm voice to wash over him scarcely conscious of her words. 'I know you'll be annoyed, darling, but I really couldn't wait any longer. Don't be too mad at me.'

'What do you mean?'

'Well, if you won't come to me, I just have to come to you. So, I'm here – at a lovely spot down the road. The landlord says he knows you all very well, because this is where you come to do your drinking. I've booked in for at least two nights – a double room. Are you very annoyed?'

He closed his eyes, and sat further back in the hard chair. Anna was only two miles away; within ten minutes, he could be with her, and losing himself in the cleanliness and comfort of her love, and for a few hours he could obtain relief.

'I'm on my way.' Then he remembered. 'But I have to see someone this evening.' His explanation sounded brutal over the telephone. 'I have to tell a young wounded pilot that his friend is in hospital, terribly burned, perhaps blind, perhaps a cripple.'

144

Anna answered quietly. 'I'll come with you darling, if it'll be any help.'

Perowne talked to Joe, sitting on the farmhouse step, and for a while Anna took Susie into the orchard. The sunset had almost finished, but the light still lingered to etch the delicate foliage of the apple-trees against the sky, and to catch the fairness of Susie's hair as she walked in front of Anna. She turned suddenly. 'It's Simon, isn't it?'

'Yes.'

'I've only met him twice. He seemed so strong.'

'Teddy says he's recovering. He'll be all right.'

Susie looked up swiftly, and Anna could see the directness in her blue eyes, then she turned and began to walk slowly through the trees again. Anna stood for a moment, watching and noting the grace of her movements, half girl, half woman. 'My God, she'd make a superb painting,' she said to herself. Later, they paused to sit on a log, and Anna continued to study the girl as she sat with her long brown legs straight and apart, hands in her lap, skirt round her knees, a pebble necklace swinging away from her young breasts. Susie shivered. Anna said, 'Come on, let's go back now,' and Susie let Anna take her hand as they walked towards the farm through the darkening trees.

'I don't think I could bring myself to see Simon,' said Joe. He still sat on the step, with Susie beside him now, and his words were the first since Perowne and Anna had left five minutes before. 'He must have been terribly burned. It's something we dread even more than being killed.'

Susie waited for him to say more, but he lapsed into silence. She didn't look at his face. 'You've told me how

145

brave he is – perhaps he's brave enough to get better.'

'Not if he can't fly. Being stuck on the ground will kill him. I know it will. And if this has happened to Simon, of all people, what chance is there for the rest of us?'

Susie heard the sound of the van turning off the main road. Joe stood. 'Come on, let's cheer up a bit before Peter gets here. He thought the world of Simon.' He added, 'It's going to be hellish lonely without him Susie.'

Luftwaffe attacks dwindled next day, despite good weather, and the respite enabled emergency repairs to be continued on the airfield. Raids were resumed the following afternoon, and Perowne returned from his second sortie to see fresh smoke drifting from the squadron base, although the Luftwaffe had failed to inflict significant damage on the landing area. Also, this Sunday afternoon, further bombs fell on houses in London's south-east suburbs; Perowne no longer knew if Anna was more safe at the 'Bluebell', down the road from the airfield, or if it would be better for her to return to Chelsea. He spent two hours with her each evening, abandoning the effort to keep apart, yet this surrender had come too late, since his weariness continued to separate them. He felt so deathly tired. Three more replacements arrived at noon next day, a Monday, but Peres was still missing, and had to be presumed lost; a body discovered in the wreckage of a Spitfire near Sevenoaks had now been identified as that of Johnny Wright, who had failed to return after his sortie on 10 July, and who had long since been considered dead by Perowne. Two of the latest replacements seemed even younger than previous newcomers, although the third, Sergeant Osborne, had been transferred from a Midlands squadron, and seemed reasonably experienced: he might survive longer. The

146

squadron strength stood at eight – nine when Joe returned, if none went in the meanwhile. So far, the flow of new Spitfires had continued to be satisfactory.

Joe telephoned the hospital each day. Simon seemed to be recovering quickly, but refused to see visitors, and Joe felt relief at both scraps of information. His own wound had almost healed. Soon he would return to the war, and he viewed the prospect with numbed emotions. He listened to the BBC news, and behind the calm reassuring tones of the announcer, he could guess the chaos being inflicted on Fighter Command airfields, and the exhaustion being suffered by the pilots. He said nothing to the family. Peter insisted on believing that the Luftwaffe raids were achieving no purpose, and his father appeared to think the same. Joe noticed Susie watching him as he listened to the bulletins and to the praise given to the pilots, and he tried to be cheerful in response, but knew he would never convince her. He wanted her comfort, yet tried to keep himself apart. One evening the wireless reported a speech by Churchill to Parliament earlier in the day. 'Never in the field of human conflict was so much owed by so many to so few.' Joe wondered how Simon would have reacted to the glowing words, and guessed his friend would have made a wry comment such as 'and for so little'.

It seemed to Joe that his life was ebbing each day, for each day brought him nearer to returning to the squadron. For the moment, he could view death almost with detachment: he would simply be gone. But the factors and happenings which lay before this dismissal of his life caused pain – not so much the thought of dying through wounds or fire, but ordinary domestic details. He ate his food at the kitchen table in the farmhouse, and he knew he would be there to eat the evening meal,

147

and he also knew that soon he would have no such guarantee of continuity: he would force down the insipid RAF food in the mess, not knowing if he would ever sit at that table again. He lay in bed at night, awake into the early hours, listening to the comforting creaks of the old house and feeling the softness of the flock mattress beneath him; he knew that soon he would be trying to sleep in his room at the squadron, with the mattress unyielding, the sheets cold and always seeming slightly damp, tucked in too tightly at the corners like a hospital bed, impersonal, seemingly only waiting for him to go, and for the next temporary occupant to arrive. And Simon would no longer be there.

Joe returned to the squadron with the comparative respite still continuing. When the RAF vehicle arrived to fetch him, he appeared to be cheerful, tousling Peter's hair as the boy handed him the small case, and kissing Susie's mother on the cheeks. He opened the car door, and seemed about to call his dog, then he turned to Susie. 'Can you keep Mops here with you?'

'Of course.' She bent to hold the puppy, and didn't ask the reason. 'I'll see you soon,' he said, and Susie smiled up at him, but his words were meaningless.

A few minutes later, Susie walked into the spare room where Joe had slept. A book lay on the bedside table – a small, red book of poetry; she saw that he'd written her name, nothing more, on the inside cover. That night, Mops went into the empty bedroom, and merely whined when Susie tried to persuade her to leave. Susie remembered the hollowness of that same bedroom when her grandfather had died, and they'd taken his body downstairs for the funeral. She left the dog in the dark, with the door opened, and tried to sleep in the blackness of her own room. She dozed, then woke again

148

to feel Mops jumping on the bottom of her bed; she reached down and stroked the puppy's head, and felt the dog's tongue wet against her fingers. Susie tried to sleep again and failed, so she switched on the light and picked up the book of poetry, smoothing her hand over the leather cover before opening the pages. The first poem she read was about love; her eyes glanced over another, and then strayed to the lines of a third:

'Brightest and best of the Sons of the Morning!
Dawn on our Darkness and lend us thine Aid . . .!'

She reached over quickly and switched out the light and, at last, allowed her tears quietly to flow.

The lull ended at 12.30 pm next day. Radar stations detected enemy aircraft assembling at a number of points from Dunkirk to Boulogne; bombers in the first attacking wave penetrated the defensive network in the Manston area, while Perowne's pilots were refuelling from an earlier, abortive sortie, and Manston airfield was reported to have received extensive damage. Perowne led one section up as soon as the Spitfires were ready, Lex following with the remaining two Spitfires, fifteen minutes later.

Joe had been placed 'off state'. He entered the hangar where his aircraft stood, once more ready for him to fly, and he climbed into the cockpit for a moment. She seemed to be waiting for him. He fingered the controls and whispered, 'Soon, we'll be off again.' Then, he walked into the sun and sat on the grass as he waited for the others to return. Twice, it seemed as if the airfield was about to be attacked when bombers were reported approaching, but thick purple smoke from the east revealed that the neighbouring base had been selected as the target.

One by one, the Spitfires came back, their wings black

149

from their cannon-fire, some with holes punctured by enemy bullets. Joe noticed the exhaustion of the pilots as they heaved themselves from their cockpits, and the way in which they stood silent in the mess that evening, some of them strangers to him. Perowne was with Anna. Joe's own solitude seemed all the greater, but soon he would be one of them again. He shared his room with young Phil Brookes, who lay on his bed fast asleep in his clothes when Joe entered, and who uttered startled apologies when Joe woke him. Simon's belongings were still scattered around, his toothbrush still in the mug, and Joe didn't want to tidy them away.

More bombs fell on London that Saturday night, with Perowne being informed next morning that damage had been inflicted in the suburbs of Islington, Tottenham, Millwall, Finsbury, Stepney, East Ham, Leyton, Coulsdon and Bethnal Green. Bombs had also fallen in the City of London itself, at London Wall and Fore Street. George continued to insist that the raids on the capital had still to form part of a deliberate, all-out policy. 'They can manage more than that,' he told Perowne. 'No, it's still us they're after.'

Clouds returned during the Sunday morning, although Lex scrambled with Henny and Phil Brookes after radar reported raiders heading towards Dover; the section returned with no success, and it seemed the enemy action might have been a feint. The wait continued into the afternoon, with the weather gradually improving. Reports were being received of heavy action in the Portland/Poole/Exeter area when the order to scramble sent Perowne aloft with two sections.

Joe flew as Perowne's Number Two. For the first few miles, he felt almost happy as they sped across Kent: he was with his aircraft again, and she responded immediately to his touch, and he wanted to take her away on

150

their own. Unlike him, she seemed ready for battle again. The perspex in front of him seemed unusually clean, until Joe remembered that the cockpit cover had been replaced following the damage to the original, and he missed the familiar scratches, and the small blemish just above his head, which he'd often mistaken for the dot of a distant aircraft when searching for the enemy.

Perowne had noticed Joe's eagerness when he sat in his aircraft next to him on the field, waiting for the signal from Control for the take-off: he thought for a moment that Joe's excitement was caused by the prospect of fighting. 'I hope to goodness he hasn't any stupid ideas about revenge for Simon,' he muttered to himself.

They met the enemy at Dover: three layers of bombers, with 109s in close escort. Perowne's Spitfires were joined almost immediately by Hurricanes from Biggin Hill, and within sixty seconds the dogfights were littering the sky, and Joe was flinging his Spitfire after Perowne in the attempt to guard the Squadron-Leader's tail. His fear returned with fresh violence, subsiding slightly in the chaos of battle, then rippling over him again as they returned to the airfield. Perowne spoke: 'Hello, Piper Two. Well done, Joe. You haven't lost your old touch.' Joe could only trust himself to wave from his cockpit in reply.

Susie stood in the corridor at East Grinstead hospital, waiting for the nurse to take her to Simon. Her motives for coming were mixed and difficult for her to understand. Being with Simon would somehow provide another link with Joe; seeing his wounds might help her prepare the way for similar injuries to Joe; increasingly, she felt a captive at the farm, with the war all around her and with Joe so closely involved, and yet with herself obliged to be apart – as if there were an unbreakable glass screen between them. Visiting Simon might allow her to open this window.

The nurse led Susie down the corridors, laughing and teasing the men as they passed; some of these were patients on crutches and others in wheelchairs, all of them heavily bandaged. Susie followed the nurse into a ward and towards the bed in the far corner. 'Simon is our favourite,' called the nurse over her shoulder. 'He'll be pleased to see a pretty face.' As they walked towards the figure in the bed, Susie felt rising apprehension. The head was swathed in bandages, completely covered; then he turned his face, and Susie saw his eyes and mouth as openings in the thick plaster mask.

'My God,' said Simon. 'They didn't tell me.'

'We left it as a surprise,' said the nurse, 'or we knew you'd be stupid and refuse to see her.' She smiled at Susie. 'Don't stay too long love – we'll come and turf you out when our jealousy gets too big for us. And you behave, Simon.'

'Hello,' said Susie.

'Sit down, and for goodness sake, let me look at you.'

She sat by the bed close to his pillow; she recognized his eyes as he looked up at her. 'God, you're prettier than ever. A cup of fresh water, that's what you are.'

'You'll make me blush.'

'Then you'll be even more beautiful. It's a good job for you that I can't move much.'

Susie found it difficult to make him talk about himself: no, it didn't hurt so bad, and he was very comfortable; yes, they looked after him well – especially the brunette. And he insisted he would soon be out. 'Another week or so. Mind you, I'll still look a bit of a mess, but I wasn't much to look at before, was I? The old broken nose and battered teeth. Who cares? Nobody looks at you when you fly.'

'Fly?'

'Of course. Give me a fortnight or three weeks, and I'll be showing young Joe how to do it properly. Now tell me – how is the young pipsqueak?'

Susie repeated Simon's words to the nurse as they stood in the corridor a few minutes later. 'He keeps saying he's going to fly. But, of course, they'll never let him. He's got real guts that one. He's still a frightful mess under those dressings – three fingers have gone from his right hand, one ear, and he'll never be able to walk easily. We thought his eyes would be dead, but the doctor saved them. No, he'll never fly – though God help whoever has to tell him so.'

Susie walked down the steps and into the garden, still tasting the faint trace of antiseptic on her lips from kissing Simon goodbye.

Enemy daylight activity lessened again for twenty-four hours, to be replaced by night attacks on Plymouth, Bournemouth, Coventry and other areas; but the strain continued for the squadron. Fighter Command Intelligence reported on 25 August that Luftwaffe intentions were still to draw out all Fighter Command resources. Perowne blessed the fact that his pilot strength had crept up to nine with Joe's return. Contrary to his expectations, young Phil Brookes had managed to reach his twenty hours of Spitfire flying. But Perowne felt increasing concern about his men's morale. As he told Anna, 'They're too tired even to get drunk.' She made no reply, knowing his own exhaustion as he lay beside her in the hotel bedroom, barely able to summon strength to talk. Only a few minutes before, she had asked him if she should continue to stay at the 'Bluebell' or go back to London, since she saw so little of him. 'I need you,' he replied, and that seemed sufficient answer.

Raiders returned in strength early the following afternoon. The first main assault came soon after midday,
directed at the Folkestone region; but interception was
carried out by squadrons from Biggin Hill, and few
enemy bombers penetrated far inland. Perowne's sections continued to wait. About 3 pm, German aircraft
swept over the Channel again on a wider front, extend-
ing north of the Thames; Perowne's Spitfires were
scrambled a few minutes later, and were directed towards Manston, with the babble of R/T talk revealing
other action taking place over the Thames Estuary.

This time, Joe flew Number Two to Lex, in the part-
nership which had become familiar before Joe's wound,
and which he'd come to dread. Lex seemed just as reckless as before, still anxious to be an ace, and still proud
of his kills even though other pilots – notably Perowne –
had ceased to speak of their own scores.

Joe glanced in his mirror: behind, he could see the
second pair in the section – George and Henny – weaving backwards and forwards to provide extra cover.
Then Control came through. 'Hello, Piper Orange. Bandits to your port. Bandits to your port. Closing rapidly.
Over.' Joe heard Lex acknowledge. 'OK, Zona. We're
on our way.' Almost immediately, the enemy aircraft
emerged line astern from the thin cloud below the four
Spitfires – twin-engined Heinkel 111s. Lex shouted,
'Tallyho! Stick with me, Joe!', and his Spitfire rolled
into a dive, with Joe about seventy-five yards behind.

As his aircraft dropped, Joe saw the Heinkels pulling
round into a defensive circle, one aircraft behind the
other, so that each would guard the rear of the aircraft
in front; he pushed forward the safety-catch, and eased
the stick away from him until the Spitfire approached the

vertical, and his eardrums began to roar with the pressure. Ahead of him, Lex had begun to fire. Joe saw his Spitfire converging on a Heinkel in the circle, tracer streaking towards the enemy but with no apparent result. Then suddenly, the bomber loomed in front of Joe's own cockpit with enemy fire racing upwards, and he'd flashed through to the clear sky below. Lex had already begun his upward swoop. 'Hello, Orange Two. Hello, Orange Two. I'm going to get inside that blasted circle.'

Even as Lex's words came over the R/T, Joe could see the section leader's Spitfire banking in an attempt to penetrate the Heinkel ring from the side: if successful, Lex would be able to engage each enemy aircraft in turn as they swept by him in the opposite direction, without them being able to bring their fixed guns to bear. But Lex would be exposed to maximum fire as he made the initial sideways approach. Joe whispered, 'The fool, the bloody silly fool.' He banked his own Spitfire, and he watched, almost mesmerized, as the section leader closed ahead of him.

Lex suddenly felt no fear, and in those last few seconds, he believed he had achieved his aim of pushing his terror away. He fired a three-second burst. Then the Heinkel machine-guns and cannons retaliated. He saw nothing of the tracer as it spewed towards him. Bullets shattered into his fuselage; the Spitfire bucked, and the sky swung before his vision, and then land filled the perspex, with the fields and woods twisting into a kaleidoscope of greens and browns. In a frenzy, he tugged on the stick and his feet thrust the rudder bar, but the aircraft refused to respond, and the ground whirled faster in front of him.

Somehow, he forced his fingers to release their grip on the stick; his hands felt like lead weights as he lifted them to fumble at the harness fastening. He reached up to open the hood. Wind rushed into the cockpit, grabbing him by the hair like a huge hand and pulling him from the seat; the force of the blast smashed into his body; something hammered hard into his back, and then he was free, with no more noise of the engine, no sensa- of falling, no feeling of speed or fear. There seemed to be no danger; at last, the struggle was over.

In his semi-consciousness, Lex noticed the fluttering flap on the pocket of his flying-suit trousers. His cigarette packet suddenly fell out and rushed upwards to knock against his cheek and to fly vertically into the air; only then did he realize the speed of his fall, and the need to pull his parachute ripcord. He tried to bring his arms to his body, but they no longer seemed to belong to him; his fingers were icy and numb, floating away from him like his useless legs, which trailed behind in his dive. He summoned all his strength, and managed to drag his right hand nearer, closer to clutch the ripcord and somehow to pull.

The noise of the wind suddenly stopped. He jerked violently, with his body feeling as if it were being pulled apart, then he began to swing with the sky and the earth rising and falling around him. He vomited. Fresh terror struck him, because he seemed to be about to fall from the harness, and he reached up in panic to grasp the cords above. Only now did he notice the aircraft circling around him; he immediately recognized Joe's number, and saw the Spitfire's wings waggling but he didn't dare pull a hand from the rope to wave a reply. Below, the ground became increasingly detailed. Never before had he seemed so exposed and separated from the world, and he realized that when sitting in an aircraft, he'd never felt he'd fully left the earth – instead, he had merely felt enclosed and isolated in his cockpit cocoon. But soon, he would rejoin reality, and war would begin

156

again. His deliverance had been false, with no real escape. The war still entangled him; terror would return with renewed violence; death still ridiculed his attempts to be brave.

CHAPTER THIRTEEN

Joe reached his Spitfire as the first bomb burst among the beeches. He jabbed the starter button, and the engine clattered into life, with the noise immediately drowned by the second bomb erupting amongst the buildings. His aircraft began to move. 'Faster, faster!' he shouted. Another Heinkel swept overhead, with two more mushrooms of black smoke suddenly appearing to Joe's left as he swivelled his aircraft; another Spitfire roared aloft in front of him. Earth vomited upwards close to dispersal, and his aircraft seemed to lurch with the blast. Desperately, he sought speed for the take-off, pleading with the machine, and he knew he sought to save her, rather than himself.

To starboard, another Spitfire tried to move between the bomb craters, and Joe noted the abrupt explosion and the huge tongue of flame as the aircraft received a direct hit. The wheels of his own aircraft left the ground, touched again, bounced and she became airborne; immediately, he wrenched back the stick, urging her on, and he banked above the trees. Glancing downwards, he saw another Spitfire moving along the grass, and the aircraft seemed safe until it tilted forward in a crazy angle, then crashed upon its back.

At the same moment, three, perhaps four more bombs burst across the airfield in quick succession, then Joe twisted his head towards the sky to see the enemy as he climbed. 'Come on my beauty, for Christ's sake, come on. . . .' A Heinkel appeared massive in his sights, and he blindly pressed the button, maintaining the burst until the two aircraft twisted apart again. The horizon fell beneath him. Another Heinkel swung into his vision, higher; and he closed, still climbing. This time, his bullets brought sudden flame from the fuselage; he half-rolled, dived, and came up again, to fire once more, and further flames licked along the Heinkel's wings. He saw the bomber sliding sideways towards the woods near Maidstone. Then, the bullets from the 109 thudded into the armour plating behind his back in deafening succession, and he flung his Spitfire in a dive to escape. The chase continued low over the Kent fields until, at last, he shook free.

Ten minutes later, he landed among the debris of the airfield, finding a way between the craters with his Spitfire bouncing and jolting over the bumps of former bomb craters. He sat with his cockpit open, resting his head for a moment in his hands; his fingers were shaking to such an extent that they seemed to be tugging at his sodden hair. Perowne's voice came to him out of space and, for a moment, Joe believed the other to be speaking over the R/T. Then he felt hands helping him out, and down to the grass.

Henny had died in the bombing raid, his thin body crushed by his collapsing Spitfire as he tried to take it to safety; two pilots from another squadron had also died. Ten people had been killed on the ground, four of them women serving with the WAAF.

Engineers worked throughout the night to bring the airfield back to full operational status, and, as he sat in his room, Joe could hear the muted sounds of vehicles. Phil Brookes was absent, diverted to another base, and Joe missed him; even his apologetic presence would have been welcome. He felt too tired to sleep; when he closed his eyes, the room revolved as if he were drunk; he needed something on which to focus his eyes. He tried to work out how many days had gone since his return to the squadron, and had to make the calculation on a sheet of paper. Today was 30 August; he'd come back on the 23rd. One week. He had no hopes of surviving another. He'd made no attempt to see Susie, and had only spoken to Simon on the telephone.

Now, Joe pulled another sheet of paper towards him, and began to write, perhaps to Susie, although without conscious intent. His opening sentence was abrupt, with no thought given to the words. 'I don't want to sleep here tonight. But I'm so weary. Sick. Yet not too tired to be terrified, and I think my fear will keep me awake tonight, and the hours will creep until tomorrow, too slowly yet too fast, because I don't want tomorrow ever to come. I feel so very much alone and lost.'

At noon next day, he added more words, in his loneliness, feeling almost compelled to write. 'The last day of the month. Probably, the last month I'll live. Two sorties this morning. The Germans are coming stronger each day, still aiming at our airfields. Debenham, North Weald and Detling were attacked first, then we were engaged near Eastchurch, and couldn't stop the bombers getting through. All the time, the R/T spewed out the voices from fighting all over Kent. It seemed as if all the squadrons were up, yet the Huns kept coming. My Spit stinks from her over-heated engine, and from my fear. I hope to God she stands the strain better than I. She must. I know I'll break first. I'm broken now. I rely so much on her to see me through each hour. My hands are still shaking, and my throat is so dry that it hurts to swallow. And only half the day has gone. The skies are clear. They'll be coming again this afternoon.'

The scribbled words were continued later. 'Twice more we flew, my Spit and I. Two more times up into those knots of streaming tracer and rushing black shapes and spinning horizons. She took me on when I wanted to pull myself away; she carried me into the fight when I wanted to seek the empty sky. I blessed her and cursed her. Save me. You would if you could, and you're braver than I. You'll go where I take you – lead me, instead. Please lead me. Rest and try to sleep. I live in you, and you in I. Rest now, for a while. . . .

'Dawn has just broken over us. Is it the last? Are you ready? Are you strong enough to carry us both? I long for loneliness to share with you, infinity, for the feel of you alone, your body beneath me and around me to give me shelter and softness and warmth. To be unborn in you. Simon still breathes. Do I? Do you?'

As he sat by the dispersal hut the sun warmed his face. He didn't want to fly nearer to the brilliance. His thoughts continued to jumble in his mind. 'They'll be waiting up there. Must I go? My life or death makes no difference. So why should I go? The sun will scorch us up. The telephone will ring. We'll have to go. If only I could think of a way out for us – some reason why I shouldn't move across those few yards of grass. If I'd lost a leg the last time, then I would be safe. I'd give in now. But then, you'd have to go without me. You're waiting for me, so close. Do you want me? To have bullets tearing into my flesh which is also yours? The telephone will ring, and you'll have to take me to the sun.'

Ten minutes later, the three Spitfires rose from the airfield, with the sunlight striking like flames from the wings. Lex led, Joe followed, George flew third. Control ordered them to patrol in the Sheerness area, where another wave of bombers was expected to make a landfall. Hurricanes from North Weald were already on station. Lex maintained a low altitude, and the shadows of the Spitfires careered over the hop-gardens and farms, the roads and the villages, over the houses of Maidstone and the silvery Medway, over the golden slopes of the North Downs, and onto Sittingbourne, and the first coastal creeks. Lex began to climb over the Isle of Sheppey, and the shadows of the aircraft left the land to sever final contact with earth.

George spoke the first words since leaving the airfield. 'Hello, Orange Leader. Hurricanes above.' Lex acknowledged. The patrol began above the mudflats bordering the Thames Estuary.

'Hello, Piper Orange. Bandits 40-plus approaching your location seawards. Arrival estimated four – repeat four – minutes.'

'OK, Zona.'

'Hello, Piper Orange. Bandits, same group, arrival immediate – repeat immediate. You should have sighting.'

'OK, Zona. I see them. Tallyho!'

A zigzag line of aircraft had appeared to the east, with smaller dots above them – Dorniers escorted by 109s – and the Spitfires and Hurricanes climbed towards them, with the two groups rapidly converging over the wide Thames Estuary.

Joe felt icy cold, his fingers clammy as they clutched the stick, his feet lifeless on the rudder bar, and already his body seemed dead. He heard Lex speak again. 'Dive! Dive!' Dimly, he saw the Spitfire in front of him half-roll and drop from his vision for a moment, before he undertook a similar manoeuvre to follow, and below them lay the bombers. Momentarily, he wondered why Lex paid no heed to the 109s which still must be above, yet his numbed brain dismissed the thought as if the danger were of no consequence.

The bomber grew larger in his sights. Now, his Spitfire vibrated as the bullets spat from the Brownings, though he had no awareness of pressing the button, and

162

he could see the white faces of the German gunners as he drifted down upon them, then the flames which enveloped their faces. The Spitfire still flew onwards, but now with only the sea below.

Lazily, slowly it seemed, he began to climb after Lex again, his limbs floating without sensation of touching the controls, and he saw Lex in front of him, and another bomber beyond. He banked to join the chain. The Dornier dropped with smoke from the wings, and with Lex in pursuit, and once again, the glittering pewter sea filled his blurred vision. Lower went the lamed bomber, Lex still firing, and now the waves curled beneath them as the Dornier levelled in its attempt to escape; Joe only knew he must keep with Lex, and guard him as they sped out to sea.

George watched them go as he flew above and behind. Even while he glanced about him for possible danger to himself, his quick brain collected and sorted the facts. Lex was a fool to go out to sea; Joe was as big a fool to follow. He himself had two choices. He could join them, and attempt to give protection from the dangers lurking out from the land, or he could stay, and continue the fight against the bombers. Within four seconds, his brain had digested the alternatives and supplied the answer, which he accepted immediately. He banked his Spitfire to plunge back into the dogfights still filling the sky near Sheerness. Joe and Lex would have to manage alone.

The crested waves continued to speed silently below the hunted and the hunters. The Dornier refused to die. Joe's mind still concentrated on the single thought – to keep with his section leader. Five miles out into the open estuary, the Messerschmitts swooped into the attack. Joe failed to see them come from behind him, where they'd

163

been lurking in the setting sun. Bullets hammered into the armour plating behind his seat, and the shock jolted his mind into action. Above him, three 109s roared to engage Lex in front, using the superior speed of their dive to close the distance between the two Spitfires. Joe shouted into the R/T, 'Behind you! Lex!' At the same moment, he kicked the rudder bar to twist onto his back; he pushed forward the stick and began to climb. His Spitfire shivered as bullets shredded into the port wing, but the aircraft continued to rise; he glanced over his shoulder to see more Messerschmitts diving below him, and Lex's voice came over the R/T again, at last screaming the admission of terror which he'd hidden so long. 'Oh God help me! Oh God help me! I'm going to die.' Then a sudden screech like that of a hare caught by the dogs, then silence save for the sobs which Joe knew to be his own.

Joe looked down. The Spitfire had gone, and the Messerschmitts and the Dornier were dwindling to the east. As he slowly banked to the west, his brain dulled again. He scarcely noted the changed beat of his aircraft's engine. Vaguely, the smell of burning reached him; his eyes dropped to the instrument panel, to observe without shock the rising engine temperature and sinking oil pressure. The sea stretched barren below, and no trace of land smudged the western horizon. He whispered to himself and to his Spitfire. 'I'm not afraid. I don't feel anymore. Fear has burned away my brain and my heart, and I'm no longer a man. I don't think and feel as a human or as an animal. My heart doesn't beat. I'm just a machine. Do you still have a heart? Does it beat for both of us?'

Slowly, the sinking sun washed the cockpit with crimson. Joe closed his eyes and the Spitfire sighed onwards, drifting lower, and the crimson began to fade into grey. The aircraft dropped into the pit, and the coldness of death crept over the pilot; the Spitfire settled deeper, and the grey became black, and Joe seemed to be entering the grave.

Colours split the black – dancing reds and yellows and greens, twisting in circles and rings and rippling waves. The Spitfire's sigh became a roar, and then subsided into total silence. The aircraft no longer drifted; instead she jerked, as if struggling for breath to take her those few yards further into oblivion. Joe felt no pain, no sensation, nothing; an unearthly calm and the final sleep.

Colours blended into black, and the black into grey, first sombre then filtering like the fog, until the mist lightened still further into clouds, and the sun seemed about to shine through. Joe felt himself being tugged, and he attempted to struggle; words jumbled in his mind and he tried to force them into sound. 'No, I mustn't leave her. Let me stay. Let me be with her.' Instead of his own voice, he could hear another, echoing through his mind, first like the insistent slap of waves, then becoming more distinct and forming into snatches of sentences. He quietened for a moment, and attempted to hear, until the tugging began again and he struggled once more.

'Keep quiet . . . How do you feel? . . . Lie still . . .'

'I mustn't leave her. I'm only safe in her.'

'You're safe now.'

'Where?'

'Don't talk. Try to sleep. This will help.' The black curtain dropped, and it seemed it would be for ever.

Light gradually shone into Joe's mind, and the grey brightened to white, laced with shadows. He wanted to lift his fingers and trace the shadowy patterns; instead, he felt his hand held, and he clutched hard in return, to

165

keep down the sickness which boiled in his throat. Blurred shapes moved in front of him and became people, and he slept again.

Perowne met Susie in the hospital corridor. 'I'm glad you could come,' he said. 'I've just been in to see him.'

'How is he?'

'Better. Severe concussion and bruising, but nothing worse.'

'What happened?'

'He came down on the mudflats near Foulness. Luckily, some shrimpers saw him land – they say his Spitfire just floated down, engine gone, to touch at the edge of the sea. The shallow water stopped him – another few yards either way, and I'm afraid he'd have drowned or crashed. As it was, I don't know how he managed to stop the Spit from turning over – the aircraft was a terrible mess. But he always was a good flyer.'

Joe smiled as Susie entered the room. He lay still, the sheets tight around him, the bandage neat around his forehead, and his hands resting quietly on the drab counterpane.

'Did I wake you?'

'It wouldn't have mattered if you did.'

'Does it hurt?'

'No. I never felt anything, all the time.'

'Teddy's just told me about it.'

'She saved me, Susie. I didn't do anything. She brought me back, but she killed herself. Perowne says she'll never be fit to fly again.'

Susie tried to talk of other things – of the farm, and Peter, and of another visit from Perowne's wife. 'She's very friendly, and lonely.' Susie smiled and added, 'She says she wants to paint me. She insists on doing some sketches.'

'I'd like that.' He reached up, and took the pebble which still swung from her neck, and held the stone for a moment, as if warming it in his hand. 'I'll soon be back, Susie.'

She shook her head. 'Surely, not yet.'

'Yes, I want to, now. Otherwise, there wouldn't be any point to it all. Why else should she save me? Don't you see, Susie?'

She nodded, slowly, because she'd no other choice.

Joe returned to the squadron only six days later. He walked out of the hospital that Saturday morning, despite the protests of doctors and nurses, and he arrived at the airfield during the mid-afternoon. Perowne and the remainder of the pilots were waiting at dispersal. So far, the day had been relatively quiet, after another desperate week during which attacks had continued against airfields. Chapman had died the previous evening when his Spitfire crashed into houses near Tonbridge; the squadron strength would stand at seven when Joe moved 'on state' again.

At 4.15, the squadron sections were ordered up after radar detected a wave of bombers approaching the south coast. Reports indicated that the formations were unusually large. Joe watched the Spitfires disappear, then walked into the Control Room; there, he listened to the calm conversations between ground and aircraft.

'Hello, Piper Leader. Bandits Angel X for X-Ray.'

'Hello, Zona. I see them. They seem to be maintaining altitude. Course north-west.'

'Hello, Piper Leader. Indicate position please. . . .'

The raiders came on, 150 bombers or more, and this time they flew high above the airfields, leaving them unmolested. Instead, they swarmed along the Thames Estuary towards London. Soon after 3 pm, the first bombs began to fall around the Royal Arsenal in the Woolwich area, and on Thameshaven and West Ham. Perowne's Spitfires returned, only to take off again immediately in an attempt to block a second bombing wave, even larger than the first.

'Hello, Piper Leader. Bandits, estimated 300, repeat 300. Formations reported parallel lines separated 2–3 miles, fighters Angels plus 4.'

Once again, the bombers made for London. Perowne returned, this time without Osborne, and the bombers still struck. Night fell, and from the control tower, Joe could see the moon turning to blood red from the capital's reflected flames. Distant smoke had drifted down to form a canopy, and huge pear-shaped eruptions of fire rose up; bursts of closer gunfire flickered like fireflies, and searchlights bored up into the black roof, like white supporting pillars. The six pilots stood in silence, appalled by the sight of unprecedented destruction, which they'd been unable to prevent.

The sky remained dark, with smoke to the north when dawn broke next day. Enemy activity proved minimal during the morning, although Intelligence reported movement over the Channel, which indicated preparations for further bombing raids on London. Joe waited with the other pilots, and a strange aircraft stood ready for him across the grass. He felt no real fear, merely acute anticipation. Then he noticed a familiar figure walking slowly over the field.

'Simon!' Joe began to hurry towards him. Simon moved with the help of crutches, his right leg barely touching the ground; he stopped when Joe approached, and Joe also slowed. Plasters still covered part of Simon's face, lying thicker where one ear should have been; his cheeks and forehead were alternately streaked with flaming red and smoother grey tissue, and puckered skin stretched towards the temple; similar wrinkled flesh spread from beneath his jaw into the bandage around his neck. His mouth twisted in a resemblance of the familiar grin, then the lips grimaced again.

'What on earth are you doing here?'

'Shouldn't be. I'm on my way to convalescence. Thought I'd just stop off to tell you.'

Joe began to help him forward again, then thought to ask, 'Tell me what?'

'The buggers won't let me fly.'

'I should think not – you need to recover first.'

'Never. They'll never let me fly. They say I can't. I'm useless. Bloody useless.' Simon lurched to the dispersal hut. Perowne tried to persuade him to sit down, but he refused. The other pilots stood in silence. Simon said, 'I tell you, I might as well have died. It would've been better. Now, they want to put me out to grass. I wanted to say goodbye.' He twisted on his crutches to face Perowne. 'Can I just have a look at a Spit again?' Perowne hesitated, then nodded, and Simon added, 'Come on, Joe. Give us a hand.'

Together, they walked slowly towards the line of waiting aircraft, neither speaking until they stood in the shadow of the nearest machine. Then Simon said, 'Give us a nudge up.'

'Do you think you should?'

'Why the hell not? I just want a smell inside.'

Joe helped him onto the wing, and slowly into the cockpit.

'Get off for a minute. Let me alone for a while.'

Joe jumped down. Simon's head seemed small in the cockpit opening, his face bent forward as if he were in tears, and Joe turned away.

The engine burst into life, and the air buffeted Joe as

he stood with his back to the machine. He turned to see the aircraft moving, and he made no effort to hinder it, as the wheels rolled forward over the grass. Perowne ran up behind, shouting, but by now the Spitfire had begun to pick up speed, and Simon could no longer be stopped.

Joe and Perowne stood in silence as the Spitfire rose to bank above the beeches. For a moment the aircraft disappeared, and the engine noise dwindled, then the sound rose, and the Spitfire burst above the trees to fly low over the airfield before beginning to climb. The Spitfire curved into a graceful, perfect loop, and then another. Simon climbed, then spiralled down, before reaching for height again. He started to spin, faster and faster, until he levelled still in absolute control to approach the airfield in a shallow dive, and for a moment Joe thought he must surely be intending to land. Instead, Simon swung the Spitfire slowly over into a victory roll, his wing almost touching the ground, before once more beginning to climb. Joe's cheeks were wet, and he still clutched Simon's crutches as the Spitfire rose steadily towards the sun. The noise of the aircraft subsided and the Spitfire became a distant dot.

A sudden white light flashed from the sky. The aircraft had turned into a dive, the sun catching and clutching the cockpit as if reluctant to see it go, and Simon began to drop towards the earth. Out of the stillness whispered the sound of the engine, the dot became a shape, the shape of a Spitfire, and Simon hurtled onwards towards death.

Slowly, seemingly far too slowly, the dive started to slant. The Spitfire gradually levelled, and her nose lifted barely above the tops of the trees. Simon took her into a gentle curve, and began his approach to land. Joe knew Simon had tried to die and had found he wanted

170

to live; he had proved them wrong; he could fly and kill as well as any man if only he were allowed.

Thirty minutes later, Perowne led his section patrol over London. The three Spitfires followed the sweep of the Thames as they flew in V-formation 6,000 feet above Woolwich, Rotherhithe, Greenwich and on towards the Tower. Smoke still lifted towards them, and fires still glowed in the streets below, to light the way for more bombers when darkness fell.

Each of the three pilots experienced their individual reactions to the sight of the holocaust. Anger surged in Joe; he knew that if he fed this hatred, his own individual fear would be partly subdued – terror would continue to fly with him, but now mixed with even stronger emotions. And now he would also fly for Simon. To George, the sight of the devastation brought relief. He knew the Germans to be as methodical as himself: the attacks on London must be considered deliberate, and in which case the Luftwaffe effort would be switched away from the Fighter Command airfields – yet the bombing of London could never win control of the air for the enemy. Fighter Command would survive. Perowne also felt relief, but mingled with personal fear: Anna had told him she must return to London, where she would be needed. Soon she would be amidst that hell over which Perowne now flew. Yet he also knew that his squadron would continue to fly.

He glanced to right and left, to Joe and George, who, with himself, were the only flying survivors of the distant Dunkirk days. Soon, they might follow the others. But the Spitfires would continue to take the air.

The squadron would live.

And selected from the Sphere War Fiction List

The first three books in the PANZER PLATOON series by Gunther Lutz

PANZER PLATOON 1:

BLITZKRIEG!

Micki Boden was no Nazi warmonger. But in the spring of 1940 Europe was in the middle of the biggest war ever fought. And for Boden and his two-man crew in their massive, lumbering Panzer tank of the Wehrmacht's 31st Regiment, staying alive had become a full-time job.

So far they had been lucky. In the comparatively calm French countryside they'd seen little action, plunder and women were for the taking, and that was how they liked it. But then the orders came. The Allies were launching an all-out offensive in Northern France, and the Führer had ordered all available armour to the coast to meet and destroy the attempted counter-thrust. For Boden and his crew, the bloodbath was just beginning . . .

WAR FICTION   0 7221 9131 6   85p

INVADE RUSSIA!

In June 1941, the Brest-Litovsk fortress on the Iron Curtain frontier fell to the power of the Third Reich. But as the huge Panzers rumbled inexorably into Russia, the fighting men of the Wehrmacht had reckoned without the blood-hungry fanaticism of the Russian soldiers. The Reds weren't going to give in easily – and they'd proved their point by impaling the severed heads of captured German tank crews on the fences along the Panzer's route!

Unteroffizier Micki Boden of the 31st Panzer Regiment thought he was inured to the sight of blood and stench of death. But that kind of mutilation was enough to churn the guts of the most hardened warrior.

Boden and his crew had rolled into Russia to do a job. But now that job took on a new dimension – a dimension called revenge . . .

WAR FICTION   0 7221 9132 4   85p

BLOOD AND ICE

Leutnant Micki Boden was faced with a tough mission.
His Panzer fighting unit had been ordered to escort an
armoured train through the Russian lines to Zholokhov.
It was a deadly assignment, but Boden believed they'd
make it – until a devastating attack on the train left the
Panzers of the Wehrmacht's crack division stranded and
alone on the Russian steppe. And in the bitter winter of
1943, with thirty degrees of frost and enemy artillery
rampaging through their route, the steppe wasn't a good
place to be if you valued your skin. Boden's only chance was
to make it, somehow, to Zholokhov. But there he found
some drastic changes – and a nauseating, bloody welcome
that was enough to make him think he was finally
losing his sanity . . .

WAR FICTION   0 7221 9133 2   85p

A MAN CALLED INTREPID:

The Secret War 1939–1945

WILLIAM STEVENSON

A MAN CALLED INTREPID tells for the first time the full story of British Security Co-ordination, the international Allied intelligence agency of World War Two whose work has been a closely guarded secret for the past thirty years. Here are top-level inside accounts of crucial wartime undercover operations including:

The breaking of the German *Enigma* code

The assassination of Heydrich

The race for the atomic bomb

Surveillance and sabotage of Nazi V1 and V2 rocket sites

The raids on the French coast that made the Normandy landings possible

Anglo-American co-operation in the sinking of the *Bismark*

The organization of resistance movements throughout Europe

The intelligence stratagems that delayed the Nazi invasion of Russia

Written with full access to all the British Security Co-ordination papers and with the full co-operation of BSC's director, the man code-named INTREPID, William Stevenson's internationally bestselling book is a uniquely important piece of modern secret history. It is also tremendously exciting to read.

'A work of profound historical importance ... a great adventure story, wherein fact is more sensational than fiction ... more stimulating than any record I have seen about the infinite complexity of modern warfare'
David Bruce (Former OSS chief and later US Ambassador to Britain)

BIOGRAPHY/WAR
0 7221 8157 4   £1.75

A selection of Bestsellers from Sphere Books

Fiction

THE WOMEN'S ROOM	Marilyn French	£1.50p	☐
SINGLE	Harriet Frank	£1.10p	☐
DEATH OF AN EXPERT WITNESS	P. D. James	95p	☐
THE VILLAGE: THE FIRST SUMMER	Mary Fraser	£1.00p	☐
BLOOD OF THE BONDMASTER	Richard Tresillian	£1.25p	☐
NOW AND FOREVER	Danielle Steel	£1.10p	☐

Film and Television Tie-ins

THE PASSAGE	Bruce Nicolaysen	95p	☐
INVASION OF THE BODYSNATCHERS	Jack Finney	85p	☐
THE EXPERIMENT	John Urling Clark	95p	☐
THE MUSIC MACHINE	Bill Stoddart	95p	☐
BUCK ROGERS IN THE 25th CENTURY	Addison E. Steele	95p	☐
BUCK ROGERS 2: THAT MAN ON BETA	Addison E. Steele	95p	☐
DEATHSPORT	William Hughes	95p	☐

Non-Fiction

NINE AND A HALF WEEKS	Elizabeth McNeill	95p	☐
IN HIS IMAGE	David Rorvik	£1.00p	☐
THE MUSICIANS OF AUSCHWITZ	Fania Fenelon	95p	☐
THE GREAT GAME	Leopold Trepper	£1.50p	☐
THE SEXUAL CONNECTION	John Sparks	85p	☐

*All Sphere books are available at your local bookshop or newsagent, o
can be ordered direct from the publisher. Just tick the titles you wan
and fill in the form below.*

Name ....

Address ....

....

Write to Sphere Books, Cash Sales Department, P.O. Box 11, Falmouth
Cornwall TR10 9EN

Please enclose cheque or postal order to the value of the cover price plus

UK: 22p for the first book plus 10p per copy for each additional book
ordered to a maximum charge of 82p

OVERSEAS: 30p for the first book and 10p for each additional book

BFPO & EIRE: 22p for the first book plus 10p per copy for the nex
6 books, thereafter 4p per book

*Sphere Books reserve the right to show new retail prices on covers whic
may differ from those previously advertised in the text or elsewhere, an
to increase postal rates in accordance with the GPO.*

(5:79